Unforced Error

A Rep and Melissa Pennyworth Mystery

Michael Bowen

Poisoned Pen Press

First U.S. Trade Paperback Edition 2006

10 9 8 7 6 5 4 3 2 1

Library of Congress Catalog Card Number: 2003115433

ISBN: 1-59058-289-6 Trade Paperback

Poisoned Pen Press
6962 E. First Ave., Ste. 103
Scottsdale, AZ 85251
www.poisonedpenpress.com
info@poisonedpenpress.com

Printed in the United States of America

This story is dedicated to Sara Armbruster Bowen,
my beloved wife and the only person I know
who is smarter than Melissa Seton Pennyworth.

Unforced Error is a work of fiction. The characters appearing in the story do not exist, and the events described did not take place. As a work of the author's imagination, and by way of emphasizing the fictional character of the story, *Unforced Error* takes certain liberties with local place names. For example, the author is well aware, from having spent many happy hours as a boy and young man there, that the principal library in Kansas City, Missouri, is the Kansas City Public Library, not the Jackson County Public Library. The latter name was used in an effort to make it as clear as possible that I am making this stuff up.

It may be helpful to readers not familiar with Kansas City to note one particularly striking characteristic of that municipality: geographically, it is very large. Its population of 435,000 or so is spread over 319 square miles. (Chicago's area, by contrast, is 228 square miles.) To put this in perspective, if Kansas City had the same population density as its cross-state sister city, St. Louis, it would be home to more than 2,000,000 souls. Hence, the city includes a great deal of open space, and it is possible to drive for a *long* time without leaving the city limits.

Prologue

First degree murder is punishable by death in Missouri, even if the victim is an editor of romance novels.

When the body turned up Reppert G. Pennyworth would see three excellent reasons to mind his own business, starting there. The death penalty doesn't come up much in intellectual property work.

Rep later reflected philosophically on the futility of having three excellent reasons when you need four. But what could he do? Not only was the murder a tough break for the victim, but it interfered with the most interesting copyright issue Rep had seen in a long time.

Chapter 1

Peter Damon had known since junior high who got girls like this. And it wasn't guys like him.

Violet eyes with a minxish glint worth half a Byron canto. Luminous smile. Ebony hair framing a dusty rose face whose casual perfection reminded him of Uffizi canvases. Ample breasts that casually mocked the perfunctory effort of her silk blouse to appear demure. Your basic Peter Damon, with his bookish pallor, wispy, light brown hair already retreating from his forehead, oversized ears, and watery blue eyes unkindly magnified by the thick lenses of wire-frame glasses, couldn't even let himself imagine that a woman like this might be hitting on him.

He hadn't imagined anything of the kind when she'd asked to join him at what she claimed was the last available non-smoking table in the Lake Tahoe Holiday Inn Crown Plaza restaurant. He hadn't imagined it when she'd introduced herself as Lara Teasdale, had guessed correctly that he was here for the librarians' convention, and had explained that she'd come to teach PowerPoint presentations to rookie sales reps for Golden State Office Interiors. He *had* wished, for the only time in his life, that he were a rookie sales rep.

He hadn't even imagined it when she'd segued unsubtly from crosswords to hookers.

"Please don't let me keep you from your puzzle," she said, nodding at the twice-folded *New York Times* beside his plate.

"It can wait," Peter said hastily, capping his medium point blue Bic pen and stowing it in his caramel-colored corduroy sport coat. "Civil War theme, no biggie. I guess crossword puzzles are an occupational cliché for librarians, aren't they?"

"Not necessarily. I'm just an MIS specialist, and words have always fascinated me. 'Hooker,' for example."

"Excuse me?"

"You mentioned the Civil War and that reminded me. Wasn't that when the word 'hooker' came into American slang?"

"Oh. Right. Because of all the, uh, er, camp followers with the Army of the Potomac while General Hooker was commanding it."

"Exactly," Teasdale said. "I love neat little *connections* like that. Like 'joysticks.' I remember seeing an Eighties movie called *Joysticks* on video, and I'm like, am I the only one who gets this?"

"Probably not," Peter said, feeling a crimson burn on the backs of his ears.

"I mean, they once called the throttles on airplanes 'joysticks' because of the phallic association." She raised an eyebrow in polite interrogation, and Peter nodded: he knew what phallic associations were. "Then when video games appeared, they called the control rods 'joysticks' because they looked like the throttles on World War II fighters. Then someone making this B-movie teenage sex comedy revolving around video games thinks 'joysticks' is this incredibly clever double *entendre*, and all they're doing is going back to the original allusion."

"Uh, *yeah*," Peter said. "Er, hey, do you travel much for Golden State Office Interiors?"

"More than I'd like," Teasdale sighed. "I could draw the basic floor-plan for every hotel chain in the country. It gets very lonely."

"I guess it would."

"Like tonight," she added, catching his eyes and lowering her voice. "All I have to look forward to is *Sports Center* and a hot bath."

That's when Peter began to think the unthinkable. He caught himself holding his breath.

"That is," she continued, "unless you'd like to come up and show me how fast you can finish that crossword puzzle while we see if PBS or the History Channel is showing something on the Civil War."

Peter forced his lips into a shy smile and made himself meet Teasdale's gaze.

"You're the most beautiful woman I've ever talked to," he said gently. "You're the sexiest woman I've ever seen. But my wife, Linda, means everything in the world to me. It would really hurt her if I were unfaithful. I just couldn't do that."

He braced himself for a cold shower of bitchy petulance. He got a wistful smile instead as Teasdale rested her chin on interlaced fingers.

"Is Linda very lovely?" she asked.

"Very," Peter said, meaning relative to the female universe the likes of him had any business thinking about. "She's lovely, and smart, and committed, and idealistic, and just a very together lady."

"She's also something else," Teasdale said. "She's very, very lucky. Please let me get the check."

It was 7:26 p.m., Central Daylight time, when Linda Damon and the twelve million other people watching *Reality Check Live!* on Fox heard her husband describe her as lovely, smart, committed, idealistic, and very together. Though the night was warm, she pulled the sheet up to cover her breasts as she turned toward the other side of the bed and spoke.

"I think you'd better go now, Tommy."

Chapter 2

Fortunately, only a handful of the other reactions to Peter Damon's unintentionally public display of chastity need concern us.

An aide to Missouri state senator Wade Carlton, for example, thought it important enough to break into a meeting between Carlton and the director of the America's Petrochemical Future Political Education Fund with a Tivo of the segment and the results of twenty frenetic minutes of Googling.

"Librarian from Kansas City," she explained as Carlton replayed the scene. "Civil War hobbyist. Obsessed with networking libraries and public schools interactively through the web. Presented a paper saying if we don't start getting libraries into kids' heads and kids' heads into libraries, we'll have an entire generation that can't identify Appomattox."

"Where is he on petrochemical issues?" the director asked.

"Get two 'graphs on this into my speech for the Majority Values Conference and make them sing," Carlton told the aide. "And have one of the interns find out what Appomattox is."

Then there was Diane Klimchock, Peter's boss at the Central Branch of the Jackson County, Missouri, Public Library.

"Caught your act on the telly," she said into his hotel room voice-mail seconds after Fox's hidden camera had cut to a different attempted seduction. "Aces! Must chat soonest. Late tea sixish Sunday evening? Only a few hours after your return, I know, but pretty please? Ring me back."

Klimchock issued this invitation not in plummy accents redolent of Belgravia but with an unmistakably American high plains twang, for she hailed from Nebraska and had yet to see the Atlantic Ocean. Anglophilia and Anglomania had dominated her personality since her first exposure to *Wuthering Heights*, however, and English idioms dating from Evelyn Waugh forward permeated her conversation.

Two women in their early twenties sharing an apartment on Sepulveda Boulevard in Los Angeles also watched Peter Damon's one hundred seconds of fame with mild interest. The one with long, sexy blond hair was smoking clove, handling her cigarette the way Audrey Hepburn had in *Charade*. The one with short, sassy blond hair was leafing idly through typescript brad-clipped into a pasteboard binder.

"What's the title?" the first asked just before Peter came on.

"*Seven Days in May*," her roomie answered. This wasn't a projected remake of the Kirk Douglas movie based on Fletcher Knebel's famous political thriller. In this permutation she'd be reading for the part of May Greene, first woman President of the United States, and she'd have more than a casual interest in the actors who'd be playing General Donald Day and his six brothers.

Reality Check Live!' cut to the Teasdale/Damon encounter drew the long-haired thespian's focus back to the screen. She shifted her smoking technique to Kathleen Turner in *Body Heat*, for she was a well-rounded student of the cinema. When Peter turned the proposition down, she brought her cigarette to the right side of her mouth and clenched it between her lips through a long, determined pull.

"Bet I nail him in one week," she said.

"Just don't do it on spec," her roommate advised.

And finally Melissa Seton Pennyworth, newly minted Ph.D. in Literature, as it was still called at the proudly old-school university that had conferred her degree, had tuned in. She watched

Reality Check Live! strictly in the interests of academic research, the way guys in the Sixties used to leaf through *Playboy* for the interviews.

"Rep, look," she called to her husband. "That's Linda Damon's husband. The guy you're going to see about your Civil War idea. "

"Are you sure?" Rep asked, politely feigning interest as he glanced up from a brochure from Engineered Storage Products Company, manufacturer of Harvestore® silos.

"I'd know those ears anywhere. I was just checking Linda's phone number. I'm going to call her tomorrow to let her know what time to expect us when we get to Kansas City next week."

"What a remarkable coincidence," Rep said. And because this isn't a nineteenth-century gothic novel, no vague sense of foreboding nor tingling premonition of disaster spoiled his foray into the arcana of engineered bolts and Breather Bags®.

Chapter 3

Job-one, R. Thomas Quinlan figured about two minutes after Peter Damon's face disappeared from the screen, was a clean getaway. Time for all that ten-k and marathon training to pay off. Experience nourished a healthy fear of getting brained any second now by a flying ashtray, or whatever the equivalent missile in a non-smoker's bedroom would be.

He hopped on his right foot while trying to jam a shoe onto his left. Linda Damon's bravely-holding-back-the-tears expression and her whimpers about what a shit she was told him that she was already well into the self-loathing stage of adulteress' remorse. All too often with rookies in the infidelity game, it was one short step from disgust to it's-all-your-fault and blunt objects sailing across the room.

"How could I do this to him?" Linda blubbered.

"It's not your fault," Quinlan panted. "It's not a *question* of fault. I don't know, maybe I shouldn't have brought the story by tonight."

"Especially with wine."

"The wine was yours. Chelsea Tuttle sent it especially for you." Total lie, of course. But then, he reminded himself, Jackrabbit Press was a fiction house.

"I'm such a shit." This from a woman for whom *damn* was a rare vulgarity.

"You're not," a now fully shod Quinlan insisted. "You're human."

"I've never done this kind of thing before." *No kidding.* "It's just that I was here by myself while Peter is off at a resort, and it's the sixth anniversary of the first time we made love and he didn't mention it—"

"—and one thing led to another," Quinlan said helpfully, lapsing into a cliché that Linda would never have tolerated from Chelsea Tuttle.

Linda started crying like she meant it. Quinlan edged toward the bedroom door.

"Please don't cry," he said.

"I've got to tell Peter," she sobbed.

NOOOOOO! DEAR SWEET JESUS NO!

Spousal confession meant melodrama, maybe even a slap or two. This would expand Linda's life experience and thus make her an even better editor—but it would make her an even better editor who didn't freelance for Jackrabbit Press anymore. Even worse, it might lead Peter to some ghastly nineteenth-century *geste* involving Quinlan. The Civil War replica cavalry saber hanging next to the blue uniforms in Peter's closet had looked very, very functional to Quinlan. He unconsciously covered his crotch, like a soccer player preparing to defend a penalty kick.

"No," he told Linda with calm and tender firmness as he managed to master his panic. "You'll only hurt him. You love Peter and you'll always love him. What we did means nothing. It was a *fling*, for God sakes. An existential accident. A chance collision of horny electrons."

Continuing his sidle toward the door, he spotted a bathrobe hanging from its back. He eased it from its hook and tendered it to Linda, keeping his face discreetly toward the door as he did so.

"Thank you," she snuffled as she snatched it.

"I think I should make you some coffee," he said.

"No. Just go. I'm sorry. Please."

YESSS!

"All right. I'll call you tomorrow."

He slipped through the doorway. He had nearly reached the bottom of the stairs and was on the verge of breaking into a full sprint when he heard Linda come out of the bedroom.

"Watch out for the newel capital," she called. "It's loose."

Although Quinlan had thirteen years' experience as a professional writer and editor, he'd never been married to Peter Damon—he didn't have the faintest idea of what a newel capital might be. He turned around, resting his hand on the wooden sphere atop the bottom stairpost.

"Okay," he said politely.

"And wait. You dropped your keyring." Linda tossed the fistful of metal toward him.

Jesus, he thought, wondering what malign Iago lurking in his superego had let this Desdemona's handkerchief slip out of his pocket as he was making his otherwise flawless escape. Lurching to snag the ring, he heard a sound of splintering wood. An instant later he found himself holding the ring in his left hand and the wooden sphere from the stairpost in his right. Lamely, he held the latter up.

"Newel capital?" he asked.

"Yeah," Linda said, deflating. "Just put it down there. I guess. I'll take care of it."

"Okay." He made his voice as gentle as he could. "I'll call tomorrow."

"Shit," Linda said, to no one in particular.

Chapter 4

At five fifty-eight Sunday evening Diane Klimchock, redolent of Constant Comment and Dunhills, opened the door of her apartment and welcomed the Damons into a parlor—"living room" just wouldn't do it justice—that evoked sepia-toned photographs. She showed them to a pink settee in front of a low, mahogany table where tea, coffee, and two tiers of pastry and muffins awaited them.

"Peter," she gushed in the process, "you're famous!"

"Well," Peter said, "for twelve more hours, maybe."

"Becomingly modest, as usual. If we can nurse your limelight for a fortnight or so we'll be able to make splendid use of it."

"I'm afraid I don't follow," Peter said. "Er, that is, I don't think I'm in the picture."

"The Liberty Memorial Library Expansion proposal," Klimchock said crisply. "As you know, we have a very generous pledge from Mr. John Paul Lawrence of Jackrabbit Press to get the ball rolling on our hoped-for addition filled with many, many of those wired-up computers you're so keen about, as long as we call it the Liberty Memorial Wing. But that leaves eleven million or so to raise, half of which we can get from our chums in Washington if the State of Missouri and Jackson County and Kansas City and other private donors will chip in the rest together."

"Ah," Peter said with vast relief as he reached for his checkbook. "Well, Linda and I don't have a great deal of money set aside, but I'm sure that for a cause as worthy as this we can, er, do our modest bit."

"Peter, Peter, Peter," Klimchock said, chuckling indulgently. "I wouldn't dream of asking you and Linda to help fill up our multi-million-dollar hole. Your help is wanted with the public fisc aspect of things."

"Not in the picture again," Peter said.

"We need Senator Wade Carlton on the Budget Committee to push through the state's share, which will more or less lock up everything else. Senator Carlton is very big on what he calls majority values, by which he seems to mean grown-ups not being naughty with each other."

"Yes?" Peter prompted, foreboding showing unambiguously on his guileless features. Linda, meanwhile, who had yet to speak with Peter about the, ah, fling, felt her gut shrivel.

"You do see, don't you, darling?" Klimchock pressed. "You're bullet-proof! There you were on television, not being naughty. It was so touching, so sweet, so majority value-ish. You're the perfect choice to go hat in hand to Senator Carlton's committee and read our prepared plea."

"But after the statement there'll be questions," Peter said, "that I'll have to answer. And I'm not good at that kind of thing."

"But that's just it, luv. There won't be any questions. You're bullet-proof. They'll all use their time to tell you how wonderful you are and thank you for coming, and we'll have our funding."

"But what," Peter said, more to himself than to Klimchock, "if they do? Ask questions, I mean."

"Now don't get disgruntled on me, Peter, dear," Klimchock said firmly. "I need you gruntled and steady, there's a good chap, thank you very much. It's not just the expansion *per se*. We're all teetering on the edge of a post-literate age. Literacy is assailed on all sides. Libraries are the last line of defense. We're like the final remnant of redoubts defending Roman Britain against the illiterate Saxon hordes."

This simile struck Linda as an unhappy one, for she had a general impression that the first time around the Saxons had won. For Peter, though, Klimchock's argument—her ringing appeal to the eternal sanctity of Language, of Literacy, of WORDS—was unanswerable. He murmured his dubious commitment to walk point on the funding request. And all the way home he looked both baffled and miserable.

"I feel like my life is turning into a bad novel," he told Linda when she tried to comfort him.

"Almost everyone's life is like a bad novel," she assured him after a moment's reflection. "If your life is like a good novel, someone writes your biography."

That won the first grin she'd seen on him since Klimchock's apartment. It didn't seem like a good time, somehow, to bring up...other things.

Chapter 5

"You won't be at the encampment five minutes before someone asks you where your mule is, " Peter warned Rep as he made a quarter-inch adjustment on Rep's collar. "Be ready for that one."

"Meaning that since I'm wearing a cavalry private's forage cap and shell coat—"

"Shell *jacket,* " Peter corrected him gently.

"—and walking with someone who's carrying a cavalry sword—"

"Saber," Peter said.

"—they wonder why I don't have a horse."

"Right," Peter said. "For Union re-enactors, the cavalry is *almost* perfect. The uniforms are cooler than Union infantry uniforms and nearly as neat as the Confederate outfits. Don't worry about this spare uniform of mine being too big for you, by the way. That makes you look more realistic. And carbines weigh less than muskets. But for some guys the horses are a real downside."

"That's one way to put it, all right," said Rep, who had never been on a horse in his life and intended to keep it that way. "Is there an answer to the mule question that won't make me sound too green?"

"Say something about the hottest fighting pony soldiers ever see being on foot," Peter said. "After all, the Battle of Gettysburg basically started when Buford got his men off their horses to block the Chambersburg Pike to Heth's troops. Although I'm not sure I'd mention that part. A private going into the Battle of Westport wouldn't have been likely to know that detail."

"The less he'd know, the better I can play the part," Rep said. "I thought I knew the Civil War pretty well, but until I talked to you I'd never heard of the Battle of Westport."

"You're in good company, " Peter said. "It's the largest battle ever fought on the North American continent west of the Mississippi River, but a lot of Civil War histories don't even mention it. The trans-Mississippi theater was basically a side-show. But Westport was Kansas City's battle, so it's the one we'll be doing this weekend."

Peter stepped back for a critical look, appraising the uniform he'd lent to Rep and then flicking nearly invisible specks from his own.

"Ready for parade," he said. "And don't sweat what you don't know. The guys are gonna have a little fun with you, but as long as you're making an effort they'll cut you some slack. There are only twenty-two notes in Taps, and the first time I played it at a re-enactment I got sixteen of them wrong. But they acted like I was straight out of Dan Butterfield's brigade. Well, let's give the ladies a look and then get on our way. We've got a forty-five minute drive to the encampment."

"Dragoons, as I live and breathe," Melissa said a minute later as Peter and Rep descended the stairs into the Damons' living room. Rep wondered whether the glint in her green-flecked eyes was mischief or surprise.

"No mockery, please, Doctor Pennyworth," Rep said. "We're *cavalry*."

"Of very recent vintage, though," Peter said. "Right up to the Civil War this country's mounted soldiers actually were called dragoons."

"Peter has kind of a thing about words," Linda explained, a tincture of apology coloring her voice.

"If more of my junior faculty colleagues had a thing like that I might actually go to MLA meetings," Melissa said. "American dragoons. I can't wait to work that into my next discussion of Jacques Lacan."

"We'll be seeing you two around eight thirty at the encampment social Jackrabbit Press is hosting, right?" This from Rep.

"Command performance," Linda said, without notable enthusiasm.

"Probably not in uniform, though," Melissa added.

"There actually were women who dressed as men to fight with both armies during the war," Peter said. "There's a great book about it: *They Fought Like Demons.*"

"But that pose wouldn't be credible in the case of present company," interjected Rep, who made his living finding escapes from verbal traps. "Maybe you could come as a couple of nurses—say, Dorothea Dix and her little-known sister."

"The Cyclone in Calico, right?" Melissa asked.

"You just impressed Peter," Linda told Melissa.

"Blew me away," Peter confirmed. "Dix reorganized the Union nursing service from top to bottom, then promoted women's education after the war."

"A thorough progressive," Linda said.

"I'm not so sure about the thorough part," Rep said. "One of her students later said, 'It was in her nature to use the whip, and use it she did.' I don't think the comment was metaphorical."

"Trust you to know *that* particular factoid about a feminist icon," Melissa said, offering Rep a playful swat. "We'll see you guys later."

A ten-year-old standing across the shaded stretch of Romany Road where Peter and Linda lived giggled as Rep and Peter stowed Peter's saber, pistol, and bugle in the back seat of the Damons' lemon yellow Volkswagen Beetle. Rep could see the kid's point. Dressing up in a nineteenth-century uniform, heading off to play soldier in an elaborate combination of amateur theatrics and community pageant—he couldn't help feeling both silly and conspicuous.

Rep didn't particularly like feeling silly, and he pathologically hated feeling conspicuous. His mother had disappeared from his life when he was fifteen months old because, as he had learned only much later, she'd been the getaway driver for a killer exiting the scene of an unplanned but thoroughly felonious homicide during the madness of the early Seventies. Other people had been shooting at the car at the time, but those other people had been police officers so the law didn't think this was much of a defense.

Not until his freshman year in college had Rep learned that his mother had been convicted and imprisoned, and later had supposedly escaped after eight years behind bars. Much more recently he had discovered that she was still alive, living under an assumed name, and supporting herself by taking money from men (and, occasionally, women) who paid her to hit them with hairbrushes, paddles, and other objects that their psyches had invested with concupiscent significance. She was still a fugitive, which meant that on the rare occasions when he could meet her or talk to her neither could acknowledge their relationship. Understanding these major mom issues helped—but outside the tight little club of the trademark and copyright bar, where he prized the respect of his peers and the confidence of his clients, he still didn't like making himself conspicuous.

And then there was the question of what his sober, buttoned-down law partners back in Indianapolis would say if they saw him in this *F Troop* get-up. Well, actually, Rep reflected, they'd probably say, *Yeah, I'd do that to go after a client.* For that's what Rep was doing. John Paul Lawrence, major library expansion donor and owner of Jackrabbit Press and several other enterprises involving print, had a hundred thousand dollars a year in legal business that was reportedly hanging low and ripe for the plucking. Rep had partners who'd dress up in boas and bustiers for a shot at fresh billings like that.

Rep drew his own line a bit short of bustiers. He didn't make as much as some of his partners but, as Melissa sometimes pointed out, the difference was that he didn't need to make any more and they did. John Paul Lawrence and Jackrabbit Press, though, offered Rep a shot at something that he found more seductive than making money: making law.

The Civil War sesquicentennial lay only a few years in the future. Popular interest would spike upwards as the anniversary approached. Re-enactment of Civil War battles was one of the fastest-growing hobbies in the country. Most re-enactors were meticulously historical, scrupulously matching collar buttons and belt buckles and shoulder patches and everything else they used to the actual uniforms and equipment of the Iron Brigade or the 55th Pennsylvania Volunteers or whatever unit they'd picked.

Rep had learned, though, that some enthusiasts found such obsessive attention to detail a bit anal. Historical accuracy could get in the way of an infantry private wearing a gold-lined blue cloak or carrying a really neat-looking sword—in other words, of the parts of re-enactment that some guys thought were actually fun. As the sesquicentennial drew nearer and popular interest grew, Rep figured that lots of these less history/more fun types would be flocking to the hobby.

A casual comment from Peter a couple of months ago suggested that Lawrence figured the same thing. Prominent among the works of Women's Fiction that Jackrabbit Press published were American historical romances. Roughly seventy percent of American historical romances, according to Linda, have Civil War settings. What if, Lawrence was wondering, Jackrabbit Press created a fictional Union Army unit—so-and-so's Kaw River Volunteers, something like that? Suppose this unit's uniforms and equipment were plausible but not constrained by actual facts? Suppose Jackrabbit Press threw in professional videotaping and photography to attract the more casual hobbyists?

Okay, Rep had thought, *suppose all that: so what?* Well, could this unit's name and its outfits and insignia and overall image be legally protected? For historical units the answer would be no. You can't copyright History; you can't trademark the Irish Brigade. Was the answer the same for fictional outfits like the one Lawrence was dreaming up? The question made Rep's pulse race a little, for the answer wasn't clear.

Answering it correctly would mean a lot more to Rep than an extra twenty thousand dollars or so at the end of his firm's fiscal year. It would mean he'd have added something to the toolbox of ideas that copyright lawyers *have* to know. Along with Fair Use and the Parody Defense, his peers would need to master a doctrine catchily named by an appellate decision whose published version would have, near the top, the discreet notation, "For the Appellee: Reppert G. Pennyworth and Some-Associate-or-Other; oral argument by Mr. Pennyworth." That was why he was riding down a leafy boulevard called Ward Parkway in Kansas City, dressed like a Union cavalry private.

A thick tome on the Volkswagen's dashboard interrupted these reveries by sliding toward Rep's side of the car as Peter swung onto J.C. Nichols Parkway. Rep caught it and opened it to the title page.

"*Sherman—Fighting Prophet,* written by Lloyd Lewis in 1932," he said. "I am now officially out of my depth."

"Actually," Peter said, "that book has nothing to do with re-enactment stuff. I took it out of the library last week because it hadn't been checked out in almost ten years and the powers that be were about to have it pulped."

"Hard to argue with the powers that be on that one."

"You're right," Peter sighed. "It's just that I saw that book and I thought of all those *words*. Thought of Lloyd Lewis typing them on a manual Royal Underwood or maybe even writing them out in longhand, one by one, decades before I was born, caring about every preposition, pondering every verb and noun. I couldn't stand the thought of turning it all into toilet paper. I was doing the same thing you copyright lawyers do, really: protecting words."

"That has to be the noblest thing I've ever heard anyone say about copyright lawyers," Rep said, thinking about defending words like *Lite*® and *Breather Bags*®. "We do it for money, though. You do it for love."

"Neurotic love," Peter said. "God help me, though, *love* is the right term. When I say I love words I don't mean just literature or poetry or luminous essays. I mean *words*, period. Grocery lists. Billboard advertising. I love the *idea* of words. There's something magical about them."

"Wow," Rep said politely.

"I'll give you an example. Do you know who Laurent Fabius is?"

Confederate general? Rep wondered. *Brigade commander under Braxton Bragg? Reconstruction-era governor of Louisiana?* Lacking confidence in these guesses and fearing they might seem impolitic, he was about to confess ignorance when a bell from a distant undergraduate course rang faintly.

"European politician?" Rep ventured. "French?"

"Right," Peter said, not terribly impressed, as if this were the type of thing you'd expect any educated American to know. "He was prime minister of France for awhile in the Eighties, under Mitterand."

"I'll take the Fifth Republic for four hundred, Alex," Rep said.

"Now, here's the connection. Twenty-two hundred years ago, Hannibal invaded Italy with war elephants and all that stuff. The Roman general opposing him was named Fabius. He wasn't strong enough to beat Hannibal in a straight-up battle, so he fought a series of delaying actions, all over Italy, until he'd worn Hannibal's forces down enough to get the upper hand."

"Right," Rep said, as this was roughly the way he'd heard the story in Western Civ himself.

"Okay. Fast forward to the late eighteen hundreds and early nineteen hundreds. A bunch of upper class progressives want to bring socialism to England, but they don't want a revolution. They want to bring it about gradually. So they call themselves *Fabian* socialists."

"After Fabius the Delayer, who saved Rome from Hannibal," Rep said.

"Right. Now cut to 1980. Mitterand gets elected president of France on a socialist ticket. He installs a real blood-and-guts socialist as prime minister. Nationalizations. Confiscatory tax on wealth. But the economy tanks overnight. He's going too fast. He needs a gradualist."

"So he cans the true believer and looks for another prime minister."

"Exactly. And out of the entire world of left-wing French politics, out of all those activists and intellectuals and cadres, who does he come up with to bring socialism slowly instead of fast? Laurent Fabius. It was just so perfect."

Uh-HUH, Rep thought as he grinned, pleasantly caught up in Peter's evangelistic fervor.

"That's more than magic," Peter said dreamily. "That's divine. Words are the sound of God laughing."

They're also temporal, Rep thought, *and now and then you have to deal with the money-changers in the temple*. Hoping he didn't sound too crass after Peter's ecstatic outburst, he ventured a question about John Paul Lawrence.

"Is the owner of Jackrabbit Press a true believer like you, or does he just play with words for the money?"

"He's made a lot more money than I'll ever have, even with thirty thousand a year from dad's trust fund, so he must know how to read a balance sheet," Peter said. "But words aren't just a commodity for him. He got the ball rolling on private money for the library expansion."

"Good for him."

"It's even more impressive when you hear the whole story. We'll catch the freeway north in downtown Kansas City, but I'm taking you there on Broadway instead of the Southwest Trafficway because there's something I want you see when we cut west on Pershing Road in a second."

"The scenic route is welcome," Rep said as Peter made the promised turn. "Parts of Kansas City are as beautiful as any urban landscape I've seen anywhere. That's Union Station, isn't it? Where Pretty Boy Floyd bought it?"

"Union Station Massacre, right. But what I wanted to show you is across the street."

"That thing that looks like a skinny concrete silo?" Rep asked.

"Exactly. That's the Liberty Memorial. It was built to honor the soldiers from Kansas City who fought in World War I."

"Okay," Rep said.

"During the Sixties there was a movement to 'rededicate' the Liberty Memorial in what politically correct types today would call a more inclusive way," Peter continued. "I still get questions in Ready Reference about it. Lots of controversy and hard feelings."

"I'll bet."

"Anyway, Mr. Lawrence is getting naming rights for the library extension because of his contribution. But instead of naming it after himself or a relative or his company, he's calling it the Liberty Memorial Wing."

"Words wound and words heal," Rep said, nodding as Peter's message clicked. "Instead of spending his money to get his own name chiseled in granite, he's picking words that will close an old community scar."

"Yeah," Peter said. "You've gotta love someone like that."

They stopped only once the rest of the way, at a freeway exit convenience store for a last indulgence in contemporary junk food that would be forbidden at the encampment. Though he would have vastly preferred to stay out of sight in the car, Rep pulled himself gamely out and followed Peter past a Yamaha motorcycle with a skull-and-crossbones license plate into the mini-mart. They chose their Twinkies and carmel corn and got into line at the cash register.

The guy in front of them looked like he was about twenty-two. He was only a little taller than Rep, which made him a full head shorter than Peter. Elaborate tattoos decorated wiry biceps exposed by the sleeves of a dingy white tee-shirt. A woman beside him flicked impatiently through a copy of *People*.

"Tin of Roosters," the guy said to the cashier, "and a pack of slut-butts for blondie here."

The cashier slid a can of chewing tobacco and a pack of Marlboro Lights across the counter. The guy paid for them, then swerved toward the Slurpee machine. This caused him to brush against Peter, who had assumed the guy was headed for the door and had stepped in the opposite direction.

"Watch your boots there, General Custer, or you'll be late for your last stand," the guy said.

Peter backed away, raising his hands palms out and murmuring an apology.

"Whoa, get a load of you," the guy said then. "What a get-up. Halloween early this year or what?"

"Civil War re-enactment," Peter said mildly.

"That what they're calling faggots' conventions these days?" The guy glanced at his girlfriend for approval of this *mot*, then took a belligerent step forward. Peter retreated. "You a faggot, general?"

Having grown up short and underweight, Rep believed firmly in avoiding confrontation. He'd learned the hard way, though, that sometimes soft words and placatory gestures make things worse instead of better. He dropped his junk food on the floor, took three steps over to the coffee machine, and poured scalding coffee into the largest cup he could find.

"Tell you what," he said then, strolling back toward Peter and making sure the guy could see the steam rising from the coffee. "When I run into my buddy's wife tonight I'll ask her about his sexual orientation. Leave me your phone number and I'll let you know what the answer is."

"What're you, a smartass?" the guy asked. He took a step toward Rep.

"Yes I am," Rep said, staying where he was. "And not only that, but I'm clumsy. I spill my coffee when I get nervous."

"That's it," the cashier said. "I'm the one who has to clean up the mess. Pay up and clear out."

This brought a threatening glare from the guy. The cashier reached ostentatiously below the counter and came up with—a phone. He punched a quick-dial button and raised it to his ear.

"Come *on*, Lewis," the woman said. "I've been waiting two hours for a smoke."

The guy threw the Marlboro Lights at her.

"You think you can smoke when I get that chopper goin', you're one crazy bitch," the guy said. "But I'll never hear the end of it unless I let you try, so haul your ass out there and let's go."

They jostled through the door together. The cashier put the phone down. Peter put his junk food on the counter. Rep looked at Peter and the cashier.

"*Lewis*?" he asked.

Chapter 6

"*Tuscan Nights*, by Chelsea Tuttle," Melissa read from the lushly drawn cover of a paperback book that still had a hot-off-the-press, fresh-glue smell.

"Her latest." Linda handed Melissa a water-beaded glass of iced tea.

"Requiring Herculean editorial effort on your part, I'm guessing."

"Chelsea manuscripts are indeed the Augean Stables of romance writing," Linda acknowledged. "Her heroines are all twenty-three, but somewhere around chapter four they'll remember Spiro Agnew resigning or Patty Hearst getting arrested. Eyes of midnight blue on page six turn up slate gray on page one-seventeen. The darlings speak faultless French, Italian, and Spanish, but have trouble with the English subjunctive. They never smoke, but if one of them has to light an improvised brushwood torch whose tongue-like flames will reflect evocatively from the gently rolling waters of the Arno, she'll inexplicably have a Ronson ready to go in her purse."

"And Maxwell Perkins thought Thomas Wolfe was a lot of work," Melissa said. "Does Jackrabbit Press know what a prize you are?"

"So they say. If Tommy Quinlan's blarney were euros I'd fly to Paris every month. He says getting 'that stuff about Titian and Giotto and the orange roofs of Tuscany' right separates first-rate genre fiction from soft-core porn. He calls me the difference between top-shelf romances and spinster-smut."

"Maybe he's just seductively stroking you, but I think he has a point," Melissa said as a quicksilver frown marred Linda's face for an instant. "Getting genre fiction right does matter, because it actually gets read. People committing high literature these days would have bigger audiences if they cared as much about their readers as you and Chelsea Tuttle have to."

"I'm harboring a dangerous subversive under my own roof," Linda giggled. "I haven't heard such literary treason since you told the AP English class at St. Theresa's Academy that if *The Ambassadors* weren't a classic it'd be hard to tell it was any good."

"I had to do that kind of thing at STA. Once I figured out that I didn't particularly care for cigarettes or Coors, the conventional rebellions weren't available to me."

Melissa took a long, reflective sip from her iced tea. She was picking up tinny notes here and there that gave Linda's banter an artificial ring, like the trying-too-hard public politeness of a couple who've had a furious row just before leaving home. Linda, from a family of Christmas-and-Easter Protestants, had bonded instantly at STA with Melissa, whose lapsed-Catholic parents bothered with religious observance only when Grammy Seton had to be mollified. Soulmates in nonconformity from early adolescence, they had known each other too well for too long to hide feelings successfully.

Melissa decided to seek conversational ground that wouldn't risk using "seductively stroking" and "Quinlan" in the same sentence. She gestured toward a stack of typescript near the stairs.

"That can't be Chelsea's next. Is it the mystery you've been working on?"

"No. It's a muskets-and-magnolias epic—Civil War romance by an author calling himself Luther Battle, which I desperately hope is a *nom de plume*. I can't get past chapter six of my flaky little mystery, or even come up with a name for my primly plucky heroine. The only ones I've thought of sound like something Sara Paretsky would use if she lost a bet to Danielle Steele."

"Give me a thumbnail sketch of this nameless protagonist."

"Austen specialist at a toney prep school who solves genteel crimes in the crested blazer set by pulling insights from Jane Austen's sensibility. *Dead Poets Society* meets *The Preppy Murders* in drag."

"That has possibilities. You're saying literature has a point beyond aesthetic self-indulgence. Which also happens to be what Austen was saying. You're hearkening back to themes from Wharton and Hemingway: courage, weakness, love, sin, atonement, redemption. You're as subversive as I am."

"Maybe the deconstructionists will be issuing a *fatwa* on both of us," Linda said with an odd wistfulness. She turned her head, but not fast enough to hide an almost shattered expression that Melissa knew had nothing to do with resonant memories of *For Whom the Bell Tolls*. So much for safe conversational ground.

Time to bite the bullet, Dr. Pennyworth, Melissa told herself sternly. The instant she opened her mouth to ask Linda flat out what was wrong, however, the doorbell rang. Scurrying to answer it, Linda admitted a tall, well-tanned woman lugging a large, bright red toolbox with *Snap-on* stamped on it.

"Hi," the newcomer said. "I'm Jessie Davidovich from Jacks (and Jills!) of All Trades." She used the fingers of her free hand to suggest the parentheses. "I'm one of the Jills. I'm here about the stairpost thingy."

"Right," Linda said, showing the carpenter to the scene of the damage.

"Threads stripped *and* the bolt's sheared," Davidovich commented. "Wow. Oh wow, in fact. That guy on *This Old House* would be over his head on this one. Good thing you've got me instead. I'll take it from here."

"Great," Linda said. "We can go up and change now, I guess." She started up the stairs and Melissa obediently followed.

"Jacks (and Jills!) et cetera is a neat little offbeat name for an odd-jobs service, isn't it?" Linda asked hastily over her shoulder—

as if, Melissa thought, Linda felt she could hide her angst more effectively in chatter than in silence. "I found it advertised on the bulletin board at Community Christian Church, which is probably why it sounds a little left coast. It was posted between a meeting announcement for the Ad Hoc Women's Committee on Getting Past St. Paul and a report from the Ministry on Inclusive Liturgical Diction."

"How did you miss chairing that last one?" Melissa managed to ask at the top of the stairs as Linda caught her breath.

"Chelsea's bad enough. I'm not going to edit the Bible."

They made their way into the bedroom. Melissa closed the bedroom door behind them, then watched Linda pull two ankle-length, brown calico dresses from her closet. During the latter process Melissa stood serenely still, put her hands behind her back, and prepared the best I'm-waiting expression she could muster for when Linda turned around.

"What?" Linda asked as she saw Melissa's demeanor.

"This is 'Lissa, *carisime*," Melissa said gently. "The girl who puked with you after we shared our first joint and finished four years at STA with exactly the same number of demerits as you had. Tell me what's wrong."

With that, the stone wall that had been shielding Linda's emotional turmoil collapsed on itself, like the façade of an expertly imploded building.

"Well, basically," she said, dropping the dresses fecklessly on the bed and sketching a what's-the-use shrug with her shoulders, "I'm a total shit."

"Right, and I'm the next pope," Melissa said. "Linda, I'm having a serious cognitive dissonance problem here. You edit books for love of the craft. You tutor at-risk students for free. You volunteer to teach English as a Second Language classes. You tape-record books for the blind. You're donating blood in two days. You walk or ride a bike on any trip under three miles to help save the planet. Clarence Darrow at the height of his powers couldn't convince a jury that you're a bad person. As Peter said, you're a very together lady."

"You're so sweet," Linda whimpered as she sagged onto the bed and broke into soft sobs, "but you just don't know. Peter is the sweetest guy on the face of the earth, and I cheated on him with a dirtball."

HELLO, Melissa thought. *I don't think 'There, there' is going to get it, somehow. The first thing I do is listen.*

She listened for eight minutes, perching on the end of the bed as Linda poured out a pitiless self-indictment. While listening, she waited impatiently for some gem of wisdom or consoling insight to emerge from her stores of academic learning. She had, after all, spent her adult life studying Literature with a capital L, and it seemed to her that if Literature with a capital L had any point it ought to be some help here. Somewhere in between *The Epic of Gilgamesh* and *The Corrections* she should have picked up something she could use now, when her best friend needed her.

"And to top it off," Linda said, as Melissa ransacked *Piers Plowman* and Chaucer without result, "I think I might be pregnant. It hasn't been long enough to miss a period, but this morning my tummy felt really different. That's why I'm so strung out today. Peter and I have been trying so long, and if it turns out I'm carrying the baby of that scum-under-a-rock editor I'm going to be ready to kill someone."

Spenser? Marlowe? Donne? Shakespeare? No help.

"Have you told Peter?"

"No. I can't decide whether I should."

Marvel? Not likely. Jonson? Butler? Hardly.

"Do you think it would help if you talked with a trained counselor?"

"I saw Reverend Siebern at Community Christian, actually. When I went over there to get the Jacks (and Jills!) number I thought, duh, paging Dr. Freud. I mean, I'm *here*, right? So we talked. He showed me the PowerPoint slides from his last sermon—*There is an abundance of sin but are there any sinners? You decide.*"

"PowerPoint slides?" Melissa asked, as Steele, Congreve, Addison, Pope, and Dr. Johnson all struck out.

"He's a great believer in the homiletic use of visual aids. He asked if I still loved Peter and if there was any chance of the fling recurring. That's what he called it, a fling. I said yes and no and he said good and good. No s-t-d risk because we'd used a prophylactic. I couldn't bring myself to say 'condom' to a clergyman. Again, good. Then he said we all fall short and no one's perfect, but guilt is a psychologically inefficient emotion so the important thing is to validate our feelings and move on. And that took care of that. The way he saw it, problem solved."

"I see," said Melissa, who was experiencing some psychologically inefficient emotions of her own. "Except apparently it wasn't solved."

"No. I tried to explain it to him. I told him that since I'd cheated on Peter I just didn't feel myself anymore."

"But he didn't get it?"

"Clueless. He got this very understanding look on his face and said, 'You mean you're inhibited about masturbation?'"

"Oh dear." *Bronte, Austen, Dickens, Shaw, Woolf and Eliot: Nada*. "Well, that won't do."

"'Lissa, I *so want* to feel like Linda Damon again. To *be* myself again. The old Linda Damon, who hadn't polluted her husband's bed."

Hemingway? Oh, sure. Dos Passos, Fitzgerald, Faulkner, Malamud, Albee? Not really. Updike or Mailer? Yeah, right.

"Let's start by not beating yourself up any more. Penance may be in order, but self-flagellation is a bit too retro even for old-school types like us."

"Penance means telling Peter, right?"

"You're projecting. I'm not sure what I mean, but that definitely isn't it."

"But that's really the bottom line, isn't it?" Linda insisted. "That's the choice. Telling Peter would be the hardest thing I've ever done, and I can't even stand to think about how much it would hurt him. But if it would make me feel clean again...I don't know. I just don't know what to do."

And at that moment, at the last possible instant, Literature finally came through.

"Travis McGee," Melissa said.

"Huh? I mean, John D. MacDonald, quasi private eye in mysteries with color-coded titles, right. But still, huh?"

"Travis McGee wasn't really a private eye, he was a moralist. He said that when you're in a genuine moral quandary, sincerely conflicted about what to do, the right choice is almost always the one you don't want to make."

"So I should swallow hard and tell Peter."

"Just the opposite, it seems to me," Melissa said.

"You're going to have to explain that," Linda said, jumping up so briskly that Melissa wasn't sure whether she was looking at perky or manic. "But I'm going to help you dress and fix your hair while you do, because we have to get a move on."

"The worst thing I ever did was fake out my grandmother, Grammy Seton," Melissa said as she began undressing. "I didn't actually lie to her, but I deliberately misled her. Semester break of my freshman year in college she wanted me to swear I was still a virgin, as she insisted I had done my senior year in high school. I solemnly swore that nothing had changed since my senior year in high school. She'd apparently confused me with some less frisky young Seton, so she was happy."

"But you weren't?"

"Not for long. Pretty soon I stopped feeling like a clever undergraduate and started feeling like a gutless jerk who'd exploited a sweet old lady's naïveté. So I faced the same question you're looking at right now: tell her and get it off my conscience, or not?"

"Don't keep me in suspense," Linda said as she fussed with the hem of Melissa's dress.

"I talked it over with someone very wise whom I really trusted," Melissa said softly. "Ran up incredible long distance charges between Ann Arbor, Michigan, and Lawrence, Kansas."

"Oh my God," Linda said. "I'd forgotten all about that. But I don't remember you asking me whether you should tell her."

"I didn't. I couldn't make myself spit the question out. So I just talked around the issue, hoping that you'd magically say something that would make everything clear. And you did."

"What in the world did I come up with?"

"You said I should stop wallowing in what made me feel lousy and spend a minute thinking about something that made me feel good," Melissa said.

"Heavy, dudette," Linda said as she fastened buttons up Melissa's back. "If I'd copyrighted that one I'd be collecting royalties from Dr. Phil today."

"I did exactly what you said. The last good feeling I'd had was when I'd finally admitted to myself that finessing Grammy Seton's oath was wrong. *Okay, I've got me: I was a jerk.* I'd felt this incredible release of tension, almost an elation, that I'd stopped fighting what I knew was right. And I realized that was the key to deciding whether to come clean with Grammy Seton: not kidding myself about why I'd be doing it, or for whom, or whether it would do any good."

"I'd say you contributed a lot more to the process than my little bit of psychobabble did," Linda said. "But what did the answer turn out to be?"

"That if I told her I'd be doing it for myself instead of her. I'd be paying for my catharsis with her disillusionment. The harder choice was bearing the burden myself. I wasn't a slut, but I wasn't chaste, either, the way she thought of chastity. So I'd live with the knowledge that I wasn't as wonderful as Grammy Seton thought I was."

"So you're saying I shouldn't tell Peter? Base my marriage on deceit?"

"Your call, best friend, not mine," Melissa said as tenderly as she could. "Deceit poisons marriage, but so does full disclosure. In Psych 101, most of the class would give the same answer Siebern did, and I'd be in the majority. But this isn't a class, it's your life, and Peter's. You've gotta know. Just remember that whatever choice you make, I'm on your side."

"That means a lot more to me than Reverend Siebern's Power-Points," Linda said. "Now, why don't you go down and see how the repair job is going while I get myself dressed?"

"Are you sure I can't stay up here and help you?"

"No, thanks. You've already helped me plenty."

Melissa nodded and withdrew. She edged her way gingerly down the stairs, feeling clumsy and uncertain in the long, itchy, unfamiliar dress. Jesse Davidovich was just coaxing a misshapen bolt segment off the bit of a compact, hand-held drill that Rep would have recognized as a Dremel tool. She noticed that Davidovich had moved the stack of typescript carefully to the coffee table and arranged a drop-cloth around the base of the stairs.

"I'll be a while yet," Davidovich said with only the briefest glance up from her work. "Hey, neat dress."

"Thanks," Melissa said, strolling over and impulsively grabbing a fistful of pages. "I'll go out to the deck and stay out of your way."

"That thing is a future book, isn't it?" Davidovich said as she inserted a different bit, with sandpaper on the end, into the Dremel tool.

"It wants to be one," Melissa said.

"It hit me when I moved it out of the way. I thought, oh wow, I'm looking at, what, like a thousand hours of a writer's life just sitting here. Like, that miter box over there? My dad made it for me when I passed my apprenticeship exam. Took him two days, and every time I get ready to cut a perfect angle on a piece of quarter-round with it, it's like part of dad himself is right there, helping me. Just like a piece of the writer is here, ready to tell us a story."

Davidovich noisily sanded the base of the newel capital for ten seconds, then blew sawdust away from the wood. She offered a bashful smile to Melissa, whose expression suggested the surprised delight of revelation.

"Sorry about running off at the mouth like that. I just got on a roll and started riffing. Your eyes must be glazing over."

"Not at all. I went months at a time in graduate school without hearing a metaphor as elegant as that one."

"Zoom," Davidovich laughed, passing her right hand over her head.

As Melissa headed through the dining room toward the French doors and the deck beyond them, she caught herself actually sashaying in the period clothing. She was intrigued to note that seating herself at the redwood table on the deck required a rather formal bit of body language. She smiled and started to read Luther Battle's opus.

It didn't start out like Melissa's idea of a Civil War romance. No wasp-waisted belles tearing their crinoline into bandages while they bravely waited for news from the front. It began instead with a southern officer returning home through a bleak landscape in January, 1865, the war not yet over, his empty left sleeve silent proof of courage under fire at Cold Harbor. As he approaches his ruined plantation, he stumbles over a mob about to lynch a low-born local girl who'd turned to harlotry under the exigencies of war and had stooped to entertaining not just Yankees but "colored troops."

"Well, if we're going to hang her," Luther Battle had the maimed hero drawl, "we're going to have to find someone who can make a proper noose." So-and-so couldn't do it, he went on, because he was busy running a pharmacy out of his farmhouse under a convenient draft exemption while brave men were dying at Lookout Mountain and Yellow Tavern. And such-and-such couldn't either, because his son had deserted Pickett's division and he'd helped the boy skedaddle so he wouldn't swing for it; and thus-and-so had refused to sell oats and beans to the Confederate supply agents unless they came up with hard money, so he didn't look like noose-making material either. And so on, with each tough in turn skulking away until the despairing whore found herself with no accuser but the one-armed officer himself.

"I don't hold with what you done," he had informed her evenly, according to the manuscript. "But you know what you are, and you just have to live with that for the rest of your life. Just like I have to live with this empty sleeve. Your family was good people, so git back to your young 'uns and maybe some of the good in your blood will come out in them."

A bit derivative, Melissa thought, then instantly reproached herself for the academic snideness. This was a story, not a PMLA article. She leaned back and let the gently lowering Kansas City sun warm her eyelids. Could you find God in a slaveholder? Could an arm left on some blood-soaked, godforsaken battlefield atone for one man's share in the monstrous crime of human slavery? Could a man who'd fought and killed defending slavery redeem himself by standing Christ-like between a harlot and a mob? From the depths of her reverie, Melissa heard approaching steps and Linda's voice.

"The newel capital looks great. How much longer for the glue to dry?"

"About an hour," Davidovich said, "but I only have to hang around another fifteen minutes or so to make sure the set has taken and there isn't any bleeding through the seal."

"Perfect," Linda said. "We don't have to leave for another twenty minutes anyway. I'll fix a salad to tide us over while we wait."

Melissa's eyes snapped open.

"Abbey Northanger," she said.

"Excuse me?" Linda said.

"Your primly plucky heroine. Her name. It just came to me."

"Of course!" Linda said. "It's perfect."

"Zoom," Davidovich said.

"Tell you what," Melissa said as she stood up and tendered the first chapter of Luther Battle's text to Linda. "I'll fix the salad. You read this."

"Recess?" Linda asked, smiling uncertainly.

"Penance."

Chapter 7

"Hey trooper, where's your mule?"

"Halfway to Lawrence by now. I had to dismount and it turned out he could run faster than I could."

The half-dozen blue-clad men squatting around a small campfire chuckled at Rep's answer. The one who'd asked the question rose and offered his hand. Muskets leaning against each other to form a teepee nearby confirmed even to Rep's uneducated eyes that the man and his friends were infantry. Rep and Peter had already stowed their gear and grabbed a meal, and Peter had been showing Rep around for over an hour since. Peter, who seemed to know everyone at the encampment, introduced Rep around the circle.

"How long have you been in your unit?" one of the others asked.

"About ten minutes," Rep said, glancing at his bare left wrist before he remembered that Civil War cavalry privates didn't wear Seikos.

"Who'd your wife vote for in the last presidential election, if you don't mind my asking?" a third infantryman demanded.

Rep spotted the trick a nanosecond too late to keep "Abraham Lincoln" from slipping out of his mouth. The others guffawed as the questioner removed his hat and shook his head at the thought of a woman voting. The approach of an emphatically contemporary couple saved Rep from further commentary.

"Excuse me," the female half of the couple asked the group, "may we take your picture?"

"Fact is," the man who'd asked about Melissa's voting habits said, "the only picture I have here is a pencil sketch of my wife that her sister drew for me to take along when I signed up. I am partial to it, and would be much obliged if you did *not* take it."

"I'm sorry," the woman said after Peter whispered to her. "I didn't mean 'take your picture.' May we make your image?"

"Oh, most certainly," the man said with an oddly quaint bow.

All six members of the group promptly assumed studied poses around the stacked muskets while the woman cheerfully snapped off four shots.

"We'll see you at retreat," Peter told the group as the photo op wrapped up. "We have to get our recruit here a little more kit."

Peter strode off and Rep followed him. The encampment was spread over four acres of rolling pasture well north of downtown but still within Kansas City's ample borders. Some men sat at campsites, playing checkers or reading Bibles. Others, in groups of six or eight, marched and drilled. Counting blue and gray troops together, Rep thought there were nearly a hundred re-enactors here already. Most of those he saw were infantry, but he noticed a smattering of cavalry and one artillery unit on each side as well.

As they trudged, Peter pointed to an open area perhaps a hundred yards square. A row of hay bales stood at one end, while four men in a medley of uniforms stood at the other, firing revolvers at targets on the bales.

"Firing range," Peter explained. "There'll be a black powder shooting competition on Friday afternoon."

"You mean those things fire real bullets?" Rep asked.

"Very real," Peter said, grinning at the naïve question. "Fifty-four caliber, some of them. The reason I'm pointing it out to you, though, is that if you go down the hill directly behind those bales and then hike about eighty feet, you'll find some Port-a-Potties. A lot of the guys actually use regulation latrines, but I figured you might not want to get that realistic."

"You got that right," Rep said.

Another two hundred strides brought them to the sutlers' tent. Sixty feet long and thirty wide and with its canvas rolled up on one of the long sides, it sheltered merchants hawking everything from Civil War songbooks to Enfield rifled muskets and period handguns. Racks and coat-trees groaned under the weight of complete uniforms for all branches of both armies. Replicas of eyeglasses and pocket watches from the era, cartridge boxes, and canteens covered tables. The sutlers all wore convincing nineteenth-century civilian dress, but Rep noticed that the prices on their wares were right up to date.

At the far end of the tent, Rep saw a sutler and a guy in a gray uniform, standing about three feet apart and ostentatiously ignoring each other. Before he could speculate too far on what that might be about, Peter led him to a different merchant with a bristling, black beard.

"Evening to you, trooper Damon," the man said.

"Evening, Mr. Jameson," Peter said. "Private Pennyworth here thinks he might be in the market for a saber."

"Well, I don't have anything quite as elegant as that model 1840 heavy cavalry dragoon saber you're wearing with its half-basket handguard and leather-wrapped grip, but we might be able to fill the bill."

He turned to a rack behind him and retrieved a saber in a brass scabbard. After pulling out about six inches of blade, he extended the hilt to Rep, letting the dull gold braid on the plain, half-moon handguard hang free.

"Model 1856 light cavalry, widely used by enlisted men," he said. "That wrap on the hilt is very fine brass wire, not gold thread. The braid and tassel aren't just for parade. You can tie that to your wrist in a scrap and it'll keep you from dropping it. Three-fifty."

Rep hefted the weapon, careful not to stain the blade with fingerprints or body oils. It was heavier than he'd expected, which pleased him. It made the saber seem like a serious piece of military hardware instead of a toy.

"Do you have anything a bit more basic?" Rep asked.

Leaving the first saber with Rep, Jameson fetched a second model from the rack behind him. The scabbard for this one was also brass, but looked a little beaten up in places and had a few black tarnishes. The guard was narrower, and its lanyard was ordinary white cord-rope instead of braid.

"That's also standard issue light cavalry," he said. "Same weight and length of blade. No scroll-work on the blade. Two-sixty-five."

"You'll need a belt fitted out with a scabbard harness as well," Peter warned Rep.

"I'll throw that in for twenty-five," Jameson said.

Rep hesitated. Three hundred dollars-plus, after sales tax, for something he'd probably never use again after this weekend. It seemed absurd. And yet, entertaining a potential six-figure client, Rep would drop three hundred dollars for dinner and wine or basketball tickets without blinking.

"Sold," he said. "At least if you take American Express."

"Welcome to the Grand Army of the Republic," Jameson said.

While Rep was waiting out the paperwork the sutler who'd been ignoring the guy in gray called to him.

"How about a piece to go with your new saber, private?" he said. "I have a Starr Arms Company 1857 model six-shooter right here, and if you'd rather have a Colt I can fix you up with one of those, too."

"He can also sell you a genuine Barlow knife over a hundred fifty years old," the man in gray said quite loudly, in what a Missourian would have recognized as a bootheel drawl. "But before you pay him a thousand dollars for it, you might want to know that he bought it from my grandmother for six bucks one weekend when I wasn't home."

Rep glanced over. The sutler had turned his back on the reb and was holding two long-barreled revolvers out butt-first in Rep's direction. Rep didn't have the slightest intention of dropping several hundred dollars on a firearm, but he couldn't hide the interest that glinted suddenly in his eyes at the sight of the handguns. He was, after all, an American male.

"Jedidiah Trevelyan, at your service," the gun dealer said, scurrying out from behind his table and hustling over to Rep. "Just feel the balance on that Colt. Try the action once. That's a Navy Colt, but a lot of cavalry carried Navy Colts. It was thirty-six caliber instead of forty-four, so it was lighter."

"Not right now," Rep said. "I'm only here for a few days. I'd have to leave before the waiting period is over anyway."

"No, sir," Trevelyan said emphatically with a vigorous shake of his head as a shocked expression distorted his features. "No. Sir. This isn't Russia. These are not ordinary firearms. These revolvers are legally recognized as historical collectibles. There is no waiting period, no registration, no license. We can complete this transaction in three minutes." In what Rep assumed was a transport of evangelical fervor, Trevelyan had pressed close enough to Rep to count nose hairs while communicating this astonishing information.

"You mean to tell me," Rep demanded, "that I could hand you a few hundred dollars, without giving you my name or address, and walk out of here with a pistol capable of putting thirty-six caliber sized holes in people?"

"Ab-so-lute-ly. That is just what I mean. This is still a free country—leastwise last time I checked."

"I'll give it some thought," Rep said as he began backing away.

"Keep me in mind, private," Trevelyan said as he worked an ornately calligraphied business card into Rep's shell jacket.

There's no doubt about that, Rep thought, turning away so that Peter could help him get his new saber and sword-belt in place.

"We can make it to retreat with a few minutes to spare if we go straight there," Peter said.

"Lead on."

The sun was just touching the western horizon ten minutes later when other re-enactors, in Union and Confederate uniforms alike, began joining Peter and Rep near the flagpole at the center of the encampment. They came individually and in twos and threes, then without orders formed into small units in a modest square around the flagpole.

In the demeanors and bearing of the men—and, Rep noticed, a couple of women—there was an intangible something, a *gravitas*, that Rep hadn't expected. They weren't playacting. They weren't just camping out or having a lark. They were honoring history. They were trying to understand, understand what it must have been like to drill and eat and rest at a camp like this the day before you'd charge up the daunting hill toward Maryse Heights or try your luck attacking the bloody angle at Chickamauga.

A sergeant and a private marched stiffly from the ranks to the flagpole. No radio or television noises reached them. No cell-phones beeped. No air conditioners panted, and no traffic noise intruded.

The sergeant barked a command that Rep couldn't make out, and the private prepared to lower the flag. Rep didn't have a military bone in his body, but he straightened his back and squared his shoulders in a semblance of coming to attention. Peter raised the bugle to his lips.

The flag began to come down as the haunting notes of Taps blared from the bugle. Jedidiah Trevelyan suddenly seemed very far away. And, Rep realized with a bit of surprise, so did John Paul Lawrence.

Chapter 8

The two stories of sprawling New England Revival architecture occupied by Jackrabbit Press lay only three-quarters of a mile from the encampment. The last quarter-mile, though, sloped steadily uphill, and Rep's all wool uniform felt sodden by the time he and Peter finally pulled close enough to count the slats on the building's dark green shutters. A few hundred yards from the house a silo that Rep recognized with satisfaction as a Harvestore® dominated weather-beaten outbuildings.

A maid in an ankle-length black dress and starched white apron opened the front door for them. She directed them to an anteroom where racks and shelving awaited sabers, hats, and accoutrements. Peter wrote his name on the tag affixed to one of the rack-spaces, tied the tag with twine to his saber, and stowed the weapon. Rep imitated him.

They moved then into a room as large as the entire first floor of the comfortable home Rep and Melissa occupied in Indianapolis. Lace doilies protected dark maple tabletops from cut-glass punch bowls and vases holding prairie flowers. Oil portraits and daguerreotypes decorated ivory-colored walls. Tomes by Shakespeare, Emerson, Melville, and Hawthorne competed with oversized Bibles for bookshelf space. At least twelve dozen elegantly tapering candles in chimney-glass hurricanes and sconces combined with four oil lamps to provide gently abundant light.

Ample as it was, the room already seemed crowded. At least forty uniformed guests mingled with sutlers and women in period dress and one jarringly contemporary figure, who turned out to be the society reporter for the *Kansas City Star*. As Rep circulated he noticed four or five men in uniforms far too neat and spiffy for them to have spent even an afternoon amidst the dirt, dust, and campfire smoke at the encampment. It seemed absurd, but he felt vaguely superior to them, as if he'd put himself in a different class by having hardtack and salt pork for dinner while they were eating fast food. He wondered if his face had had the same wary, cards-close-to-the-vest, outsider's look when he'd first hit the encampment.

"How about a date, soldier?"

Rep swiveled to catch Melissa's sly smile, enhanced by the softer glow of the candle light. She handed him a cup of punch and clinked hers against his.

"If the Union Army had had camp followers as lovely as you, the Civil War might have lasted fifteen years," he said.

"*Very* nicely put. A few more compliments like that and before long we'll be playing Dorothea Dix and the Naughty Scholar. Should someone tell that corporal in the white pants over there that he sewed his stripes on the wrong way? Every other striper has them tips down, and his are tips up."

"If he has white pants and red trim on his collar, his stripes are right. He's here as a Marine—probably the only one—and Peter told me that's the way Marine noncoms wore their stripes in the Civil War."

"If a few hours at the encampment has left you this insufferably knowledgeable, you may be impossible to live with by the end of the weekend," Melissa said. "Apart from encouraging your penchant for arcane pedantry, how do you like the experience so far?"

"More than I thought I would. Some of the guys who were playing old soldier on me this afternoon shook hands with me just now and it made me feel like a million bucks. Us/them kind of thing. Are you noticing any subtle effects on your attitudes from your immersion in the era?"

"I'm not ready to start lashing Latin and arithmetic into trembling schoolgirls, but there's something there, all right. You move more carefully in a dress like this, and I think it carries over into being a little more polite, a bit more formal—maybe even a tiny bit stiff."

"Heaven forbid. Where's Linda, by the way?"

"Finding Peter and cutting him out of the herd."

Following Melissa's nod, Rep saw Linda leading Peter halfway across the room, toward a doorway that presumably led to the back of the house. He noticed that Melissa's expression now bespoke a dauntingly single-minded focus that he'd seen before—during the prep for her comprehensive examinations, for example.

"Something's up," he said. "What is it?"

"Oh, dear, am I that transparent?"

"Only to an intellectual property lawyer. A litigator would have missed it."

"All I'm allowed to tell you is that they need to spend some time alone with each other. And I may have to run interference for them."

"Someone has to. This isn't a place for private conversation."

"Linda has a key to the editorial offices on the second floor. She also has a minibar bottle of scotch they brought back as a souvenir from New York last summer—for courage, I assume, but maybe just as a good luck charm."

"This sounds serious," Rep said.

"Amen. I doubt she's had anything stronger than Chablis since our senior prom. Where I come in, though, is that other people also have keys. So if I disappear for awhile later on—"

"You've said enough. If you tell me any more you'll have to kill me."

"How *do* you achieve such impressive levels of intellectual penetration?"

"I married a clever girl and I have to keep up."

A hint of a commotion drew Rep and Melissa's attention toward the center of the room. The man making his leisurely but determined way toward them had iron gray hair combed with an elegance just offhand enough to suggest swagger. Rep guessed that he was in his mid-sixties. A pair of wrinkles near the jaw line on each cheek served to emphasize the overall firmness of his tanned face, while bespeaking a wholesome contempt for the plastic surgeon's knife and needle. He wore a federal blue, long-tailed coat with oversized brass buttons and a buff suede vest that reminded Rep of paintings of Daniel Webster arguing for the Compromise of 1850.

"Good evening." The man extended his hand and smiled as he reached Rep and Melissa. "I am John Paul Lawrence, and I believe I have the honor of addressing attorney Reppert G. Pennyworth and his good wife."

He somehow managed to get this out without the words sounding stilted, which struck Rep as a pretty good trick. Lawrence grasped Melissa's hand and bowed to kiss her fingers.

"This is a very special event you've arranged," Melissa said. "The building is magnificent, and you've gotten things exactly right for this group."

"You're very kind to say so," Lawrence said. "I wish I could claim that commercial considerations were entirely foreign to the effort, but I can't. Right now Civil War re-enactment is just an esoteric hobby for a fairly small group of enthusiasts. If the media start hyping it enough to make a real splash with the general public, a large backlist of period romances from Jackrabbit Press will be ready for fresh covers and republication."

"Don't apologize for commercial considerations," Rep said. "They keep copyright lawyers in wine and cheese."

Melissa spotted Linda and Peter slipping through the doorway.

"I sense a brandy-and-cigars moment coming up, so in the spirit of the age I will discreetly excuse myself," Melissa said. Exchanging nods and tolerant smiles with Lawrence, she glided away.

"Mrs. Pennyworth is quite discerning," Lawrence said. "I do have business to discuss. Let's go to my study."

"By all means," Rep said.

Rep followed Lawrence through the parlor to the inside doorway that Peter and Linda had already used. This led to a hall between a stairway and dining room on the right and a substantial wooden door on the left. Lawrence unlocked the latter and turned toward Rep as he swung it open.

"We are now officially out of role," he said. "On the other side of this door we step back into the twenty-first century."

Lawrence had put it mildly. They walked into an ultra-modern conference room. Chrome, glass, and black leather furniture. Built-in Sub-Zero mini-refrigerator and wine cooler. An iMac desktop computer in a turqoise housing, and a Hewlett-Packard laser printer. Large screen Sony television and Bose radio/CD player. Framed covers of Jackrabbit Press books mounted on walls whose pale blue linen covering looked like it cost eighty dollars a square foot. The only apparent period touches were a black-framed, yellowed document signed in spidery, old-fashioned handwriting and a very busy medal mounted on a plaque. Rep could barely make out "General Order No. 11" typeset in large letters at the top of the document.

He saw only one photograph. The badly focused, black-and-white print showed a thin, light-haired man in horn-rimmed glasses. Rep thought shackles bound his wrists, but grainy resolution made it hard to tell for sure.

"There has to be a story behind that," Rep said.

"His name was Robert Brassilach," Lawrence said, pronouncing the first name *Ro-BARE.* "He was a respected poet, a fine novelist, and a truly gifted critic. If he had lived to fulfill his promise, he might have become the greatest French literary commentator of his generation."

"What happened to him?"

"He was executed by a firing squad in France during World War II."

"Resistance?"

"A broad term," Lawrence said with an eloquent shrug. "Essentially, Brassilach was shot for editing a newspaper."

"A martyr to freedom of thought," Rep said.

"Exactly." Lawrence picked up a telephone and murmured something into it. Then he poured amber liquid from a crystal decanter into two thimble glasses and offered one to Rep. "Cigars hadn't occurred to me, but I can certainly provide some brandy. Please make yourself comfortable."

As Rep sat down, a rap sounded at the door. Lawrence buzzed it open. A man in a blue uniform came in, looked uncertainly around him, then shuffled over to where Lawrence was standing. Rep recognized him as one of the re-enactors in the parlor who had seemed out of place.

"Mr. Pennyworth," Lawrence said, "meet Sergeant Jones of the Kaw River Volunteers. No such unit fought in the Civil War, of course. We've taken a number of other historical liberties as well. The uniform is combed cotton instead of wool—no trivial matter at Gettysburg in July. Dark blue wide-brimmed slouch hat instead of a forage cap. Although this is an infantry unit, you'll notice that the outer garment isn't a sack coat but a cloak, shamelessly calculated to appeal to the generation that made *Lord of the Rings* a mega-hit. The basic small arm won't be a muzzle-loading rifled musket but the Spencer repeating rifle, which actually was used by a few units."

"All in the interest of broadening appeal?" Rep asked.

"Exactly. Thank you, Sergeant, that was quite helpful." The blue-clad figure nodded briefly and left. "I respect the purists who hope through meticulous authenticity to achieve some kind of spiritual communion on the parade ground or picket duty with the soldiers who actually fought the war. But mysticism isn't a commercial proposition."

"Right," Rep said. "After all, you're trying to reach as wide an audience as possible."

"Indeed I am. Imagine my corps as a kind of living novel. An instant publicity hook for author signings and fan conventions. Honorary memberships for readers, linked with advance notice of upcoming books. I know I sound philistine, but the possibilities are glittering."

Well, Rep thought, *they would be if romance novels were bought by guys instead of women. But maybe that's the point.*

"It's hard to argue with that," Rep said.

"So let's talk about those possibilities, shall we?"

They did. Rep began to explore the general issue of getting legal protection for what Lawrence rather elegantly called a living novel. And while he talked, half of his mind ran the numbers from the Jackrabbit Press Dunn and Bradstreet report he had reviewed, and computed the payback rate from eight, twelve—why not?—twenty titles a year.

You know what? he thought to himself. *This guy must be a lot smarter than I am. Because bottom line, I don't see how this thing can work.*

Chapter 9

While Rep's chat with Lawrence ran its course, Melissa stood outside the back door to the house, anxiously watching a battleship-gray DeLorean screech to a stop near the crown of a turnaround at the end of the driveway. She hadn't flirted with anyone but Rep in a long time, and she'd hoped that Peter and Linda would get their little chat over with before she had to deploy her rusty wiles on R. Thomas Quinlan. Now that the DeLorean had arrived, though, game time had arrived with it.

She had a few minutes to consider tactics because it took Quinlan that long to whip out a car cover and fit it lovingly over his vehicle, singing jauntily as he did so. The tune was "My Favorite Things" from *The Sound of Music*. With the wind blowing from Quinlan's direction, Melissa could pick up lyrics that departed from the original score:

> *Half-slips and full slips and pink satin panties,*
> *Black leather teddies and silken blue scanties,*
> *Thongs more exquisite than strippers' g-strings—*
> *These are a few of my girl's underthings.*

Finally Quinlan, in all of his sandy-haired, muscle-rippling, Crest-commercial smiling, health-glowing magnificence, approached the building. And Melissa discovered that all she'd need to draw his attention was to be a moderately attractive woman under fifty.

"Hi," he said, as he spotted her by the door. "Here for the social, right?"

"Guilty."

"Sneak out for a cigarette?"

"Just some fresh air," Melissa said. "I don't smoke. I'm not prissy about it, though. You go ahead if you like."

Quinlan flashed a rueful, ten-thousand megawatt grin at her.

"Like?" he said. "I would *love* a cigarette. I would *kill* for a cigarette. But I can't have one."

"I don't see how it could be a health problem," Melissa said, unsubtly admiring Quinlan's physique. "And offhand I'd guess against religious scruples as well."

"Dropped the church thing a *long* time ago," Quinlan nodded, all lovable scamp. "Got tired of giving up adultery for Lent."

"I see," Melissa said. The seduction had now officially begun.

"It's the Boston Marathon," he said. "Greatest running experience in the world. Been dreaming of it for two years. But I need to finish a qualifying marathon in under four hours to get there. There's one coming up in St. Louis next month. I'm training for it. *Seriously* training."

Well, aren't you a splendid chap? Melissa thought, noting that this was exactly what she was supposed to think.

"Daunting dedication," she said, shaking her head in ostensible wonder.

"What can I say? Listen, would you like to go for a drive? Ever been in a DeLorean?"

"Maybe not a drive," Melissa said. "But I would like to see the car, and it's very nice of you to offer."

She had apparently hit on the only topic Quinlan cared about as much as himself, for he instantly led her over to the vehicle and raised the cover from the hood and driver's side. He lifted the gull-wing door open, helped her into the driver's seat, and pointed out the leather-wrapped steering wheel and knurled walnut dashboard with its impressive array of dials and gauges. Melissa did her best to look interested.

"Check this out," Quinlan said then.

Reaching across her and brushing her breasts, he popped open a near-invisible compartment under the dash and pulled out a thick plastic bag full of what Melissa readily identified as pot. "Plastic bag" understated things considerably. Sides many mills thick gave it a feeling of substance, and no-nonsense, heavy-duty seals secured the top. If Tiffany's made Zip-Lok bags, she thought, they might look something like this.

"Pure Jamaican gold," Quinlan said reverently, pressing a bit closer.

"I hope you enjoy it."

"Would you like to enjoy some right now?"

"No, thanks."

"Are you telling me you've never smoked marijuana?"

"No," Melissa said.

"But you've gotten all grown up and stuffy and now you're ashamed of your naughty past?"

"No. It was something I did at a certain time in my life. Looking back on it, I think it was a mistake. But maybe a bigger mistake would have been living my life without making any mistakes. Why don't I get out now so that you can re-stash your Jamaican gold without my brassiere getting in the way?"

"Now, now, coy mistress," Quinlan chided, as he pointedly didn't move. "World enough and time and all that." He closed in even more, reaching across her so that his arms framed her shoulders and Melissa could guess with considerable confidence that his dinner had involved pepperoni.

"Let me out right *now*," Melissa said in a quietly fierce voice. She swung her right fist toward his chops, but she had a bad angle and no leverage in the cramped quarters. She landed a pathetic love-tap instead of an eye-opener.

"YEOOWWW!" Quinlan nevertheless yelped, to Melissa's vast surprise. He leaped back, smacking his head on the upswung door in the process.

"I think you should take that as a no, dearie," a richly rolling female voice said.

"Hey, CT, fun's fun but that really hurt!"

"If it didn't hurt, then Big Dee's Tack and Veterinary Supply Company gypped me out of thirty-nine-ninety-five plus shipping and handling."

CT? Melissa thought. *Trouble with the English subjunctive? Could it be?*

Melissa climbed out. She saw Quinlan rubbing his bottom with one hand while he cradled his pot with the other. Confronting him was a stocky woman with frosted blond hair. Dressed in full English hunting pinks and knee-high black leather stirrup boots and swishing a wicked-looking riding crop, she carried fifty-plus years with stolid confidence.

"Chelsea Tuttle, if I'm not mistaken," Melissa said. "I'm Melissa Pennyworth. Thanks."

"*Du rien, ma soeur*. I just came from a reading at the Kansas City Hunt Club which Mr. Quinlan didn't bother to attend, and I found that little flick quite cathartic."

"You never can tell when a riding crop will come in handy."

"Just so. When I bought the thing I was afraid it might be a little too-too. The only other prop that works with hunting pinks is a cigarette holder, though, and smoking is such a *dreary* cliché for writers my age. Joan Didion ruined it for all of us."

"Look, CT," Quinlan said, "I'm sorry about the reading, but you do one of the goddamn things about every three weeks and something came up."

"Keep your eyes and ears open and your mouth shut before you get in more trouble than you already are," Tuttle advised Quinlan sternly. She emphasized the point by poking him in the chest with the crop's tip. "We have to talk. That is to say, I have to talk and you have to listen."

"Talk about what?" Quinlan asked.

"You know bloody well what, you callow rotter. And if you don't I just left a note in your office that should clue you in. I'll see you at noon tomorrow, and if you have any brains at all you'll have the champagne chilled."

"Time out," Quinlan said. "I have a command performance around midnight, and I don't know how long it's going to go. I may not be out of bed by noon. If your problem is that important, let's go up and talk right now."

Melissa's pulse jumped at that comment, but she needn't have worried.

"Noon tomorrow, dear heart," Tuttle said. "I'll be devoting the rest of the night to an in-depth study of marine biology. T-T-F-N."

She executed an about-face and strolled regally down the driveway, into the darkness. Melissa stole away as well, dispensing with formalities, for as she turned toward the back door she saw Rep coming around the corner of the house. Melissa hustled over to him, fussily lifting her skirt to keep from tripping over its hem and feeling as she did so that she must look like Aunt Polly from *The Adventures of Tom Sawyer.*

"What's up?" she asked. "Where are Peter and Linda?"

"Well, Linda is apparently in the ladies' room upstairs, and Peter by now is presumably waiting impatiently outside of it. He tracked me down and told me she'd been in there for an uncomfortably long time. He feels silly asking, but he'd like you to go in and make sure she's all right."

Uh-oh, Melissa thought. She chanced a look over at Quinlan, who had slipped back into his car either to re-stow his pot or perhaps to take a few calming tokes.

"Let's go," she said briskly.

She led Rep through the back door and up the stairs. Seeing Peter pacing anxious circles at the far end of the second floor hallway, she figured the restrooms must be there as well. She scurried down the hall and pushed into the ladies' room, offering Peter a hurriedly reassuring pat in transit. She found Linda on her knees, embracing the bowl of the nearest commode and vigorously engaged in reverse peristalsis.

"Okay, bunky, it's going to be all right," Melissa said, dropping to her haunches beside Linda. She pulled Linda's luxuriant chestnut hair back and laid a calming palm on her forehead. She rolled with the motion as Linda heaved again, then gentled her friend back and flushed the toilet.

"I think that's it," Linda panted.

"Just sit still in case it's not," Melissa said.

"God, I shouldn't drink," Linda said. "I don't drink."

"I can see that," Melissa said. "Hang on a minute."

"Don't leave me!" Linda pleaded with frantic urgency.

"I'll be right back. Just sit tight."

Rising, Melissa moved first to the restroom door. Linda vomiting wasn't that big a deal—certainly not for someone who'd made it through four years of undergraduate life at the University of Michigan. Far more alarming was the prospect of Quinlan marching up the stairs at any moment. The one thing that absolutely must not happen was for Quinlan to run into Peter in the next fifteen minutes or so. As she opened the door, she hoped desperately that Rep would pick up winks and nudges with his usual facility.

"Okay," Melissa said with a no-details-right-now-please exhalation. "It's going to be a few minutes yet, but there's nothing to worry about. Something a little off in the salad dressing this afternoon would be my guess, but everything is absolutely fine now. We just need a little while to freshen up and then we'll find you fellas downstairs."

"Freshen up?" Peter asked, his expression suggesting that that flippancy strained even his credulity.

"Chick thing," Rep said, popping Peter on the bicep. "Don't try to figure it out. Let's get back to the guys 'til these two are through."

Rep began walking toward the stairs. Nodding as if Rep had just shared an insight of Kantian profundity, Peter followed him, uncertainly at first and then with apparently growing confidence. By the time they had gotten back into the parlor Peter was leading the way, steering Rep toward the anteroom.

"Was Melissa just trying to humor me or does she really mean everything is all right?" Peter asked urgently as, to Rep's surprise, he clapped his forage cap on his head and began to fit his saber back into his belt.

"I don't know what's going on," Rep said, "but if Melissa says things are fine then things are fine. Chick-time has nothing to do with clock-time, so it may take awhile. But eventually Linda will be down here as good as new."

"I was thinking of driving her home," Peter said, "but a long road trip in the next hour is probably the last thing she needs."

"I thought we were sleeping under canvas tonight," Rep said, blinking with surprise. "I thought that was the whole idea."

"Right, we were and it was. But something I need to take care of has come up all of a sudden, and I can't wait around much longer. If you're sure Linda's all right, I'm going to take off. I'll try to be back before morning if I can, but don't count on it. In fact, I'd appreciate it if you'd hunt up Charlie Rutherford and have him play *reveille*."

"One-eighties make me dizzy," Rep said. "What could possibly have come up in the last hour that's so important it can't wait 'til morning?"

"It's kind of hard to explain. I have to check something before I'll even know if it's anything at all. Just tell Linda that I know she'll understand, and I'll explain everything as soon as I can."

A quick handclasp and Peter was gone while Rep was still opening his mouth to protest further.

Melissa by that time had sponged off Linda's face, gotten a cup of water down her throat, and patted a semblance of pink back into her cheeks.

"Okay," Melissa said then. "From the top, but after two deep breaths."

"Right," Linda said after obediently gulping air. "After taking a pop from that bottle of Johnny Walker Black to get my nerve up, I got Peter to the office. I'd prepared a neat little speech, but I never got past *there's something I have to talk to you about.* Then I saw his uniform looking so perfect on him. And I saw his face glowing with unconditional devotion, and this look of boyish hope in his eyes. And I thought about him being out here to spend the rest of the week with his re-enactment buddies, doing this thing he loves so much. And I knew you were right. And Siebern was right. Even Quinlan was right."

"Not quite peer review, but I'll take it," Melissa said.

"I knew I shouldn't tell him. Not only couldn't but shouldn't. That if I did, I'd be doing it for me and not for him, hurting him for no good reason."

"I think you made the right choice."

"But then I had to cover so I started rattling on," Linda said. "I said I just had to tell him what a wonderful husband he was and how thrilled I was to be married to him. And we, uh, kind of started making out a little bit. Quite a bit, actually. When he wasn't nibbling my ear he was whispering to me about how I'm a faultless angel and so forth."

"This doesn't sound like regurgitation material so far," Melissa said.

"That came when we stopped to catch our breath. He held me at arms' length, and looked at me, and then he just lit up like a six-year-old seeing the tree on Christmas morning. His face was like *I got it! I got it!* And he said he could tell I thought I was pregnant but I wouldn't come out and say it yet because I was worried about getting his hopes up too soon."

"And you started to cry?" Melissa guessed.

"No, I was already crying. I started to feel everything come back up. I knew I wasn't just going vomit but hurl big time, like an outtake from *Animal House*. I mean, the nervous tension and everything, and then the somewhat unfortunate irony on top of it—"

"I understand," Melissa said.

"So I made a mad dash for the restroom. I thought a Johnny Walker encore might calm me down, but it had the opposite effect. I mean, dumb, yeah, I know. Totally. Except for New Year's Eve and friends getting shucked by their husbands, I don't do hard liquor at all. Anyway, I lost lunch, tea, and salad, and it seemed to go on and on. Thank God you came in."

"All right, trooper," Melissa said jauntily, climbing to her feet and pulling Linda after her. "A rough patch, but no harm done.

Time to show the flag. I think we'll stick with fruit punch for the rest of the night."

By the time they reached the hallway Linda was walking on her own, and when they approached the head of the stairs her gait had gotten downright steady. That's when they saw Rep coming up.

"Where's Peter?" Melissa asked sharply.

"Halfway to I-29 would be my guess," Rep said. He then quickly described Peter's exit and relayed his message.

"Oh God," Linda panted, a frantic desperation straining her voice. "No, oh please God, no."

"Steady," Melissa said.

"What's up?" Rep asked.

"Honey," Melissa said to him, "this is one of those yours-not-to-reason-why situations, okay? I want you to go down to the bottom of the stairs, and if anyone starts to come up before Linda and I get back down, I want to know about it before they reach the second step."

"Yas'm," Rep said, clicking his heels and saluting. He headed for his post as Melissa stuck her tongue out at him.

"All right," Melissa said then to Linda, "into the office. We need to find out if Peter could possibly have seen anything in there that would have tipped him off to your fling." *Like Chelsea Tuttle's* note, she thought but saw no point in mentioning. Yet.

Linda showed Melissa into the large, open office space that Quinlan shared with Linda and other freelance editors when they worked on site. Melissa was feverishly running through a set of rationalizations to justify opening and reading Tuttle's note, but her scruples were wasted. No envelope sheltered the missive. No folds concealed its message.

A letter-opener savagely pinned a typewritten page to the head-high top cushion on Quinlan's leather desk chair. Even from ten feet away Melissa could read the words hand-printed in scarlet lipstick across the typescript: "NICE TRY," followed by a suggestion of the twelve-letter word for *incestuous son*. (A suggestion only, rather than the word itself, for asterisks had replaced all but the M, the F, and the Rs.) "CT" served for a signature.

"The bowdlerization seems anomalous in context," Melissa murmured.

"Chelsea always has been fastidious about indecent language," Linda explained earnestly. "She knows her demographic."

"Isn't the letter opener a bit over the top?"

"Not for Chelsea. Anything short of an Italian dagger with a jewel-encrusted hilt would strike her as the epitome of restraint."

Melissa leaned close enough to the letter to read its type-written text aloud to Linda. "Dear Chelsea: I am delighted to confirm that Jackrabbit Press is prepared to make an offer for first-publication rights to your novel, *An Inescapable Courtesy*. Enclosed is a contract providing for an advance and royalties twenty percent better than our standard arrangement. As you will appreciate, a surrealistic, experimental novel involving intersecting narrative vectors linking the occupation of Japan after World War II with the birth of disco and the election of the first woman pope will represent a major departure for both you and Jackrabbit Press. Finding just the right marketing approach will be essential. I can only hope that you are as excited by this challenge as I am. I look forward to working together with you on this exhilarating project."

"Incredible," Linda said.

"It seems to have aggravated Chelsea," Melissa said, "but I don't see anything in there that could have alerted Peter."

"Then it must have been something else," Linda said despairingly as she sank into a chair and contributed a few gasping whimpers.

Melissa chanced a sidelong glance to make sure Linda was in fact moving away from Quinlan's desk. Something dull and metallic near the top of Quinlan's desk blotter had caught her eye. She wanted to look more closely at it without drawing Linda's attention to it. The five-second examination that she managed left her hollow-bellied. She saw a knuckle-sized chunk of bolt with the threads worn smooth. Three strands of chestnut hair tied around the object in a delicate bow served as decoration.

As Melissa turned back to Linda and gazed at the rich chestnut mane that Melissa had always envied she remembered Jesse Davidovich's throwaway comment about the newel capital—*threads stripped and the bolt's sheared.* She didn't have any trouble imagining a fragment of broken bolt flying unnoticed into Quinlan's pant-cuff as he caught his keys. And she could easily picture his prurient delight later on as he tied stray locks of Linda's hair around the thing to turn it into a love trophy.

Had Peter seen this while Linda was blowing lunch and figured out what it meant? She didn't know.

Should she tell Linda about it? Not yet.

"Snap out of it," Melissa said to Linda instead, with a tough-love sharpness. "You're jumping to conclusions. We don't know what sent Peter hurrying away. His comments to Rep certainly didn't sound like a jealous husband furious over infidelity."

"You're right," Linda said, shaking her head with spunky determination. "You're doing everything you can to help, and I'm acting like a sniveling wimp. You must feel like slapping me silly."

"Of course not," Melissa said. *Not silly.* "Now, let's get going."

"Where?"

"Wherever we think Peter is."

Chapter 10

You wake up earlier when you're sleeping in a bedroll under a tent than you do on a soft bed under a roof, Rep reflected, a little after five thirty on Wednesday morning. You hear morning sounds that you don't hear indoors. Metal cups clanging against metal plates. Canvas rustling. Predatory songbirds warbling in melodic triumph over lesser fauna that they've turned into breakfast. Rain dripping on the forage cap you'd put over your face.

Right, Rep thought. *Now I remember. The Port-A-Potties.*

He pulled himself stiffly from his bedroll and found his boots stowed upside down on sticks stuck in the spongy earth. Peter's bedroll a few feet away lay snugly tied and clearly unused. Had Peter shown up, Rep's instructions were not to let him out of his sight pending contact with Melissa or Linda. *So much for that*, Rep thought—with relief rather than anxiety, for he didn't share the wives' edginess about Peter's exit. He viewed it, in fact, as gender-specific overreaction. Stuff happens, for crying out loud.

Rep hesitated about wearing his saber to the john, then decided that he felt less ridiculous with it than without it. Ducking under the tent flap into a fine mist, he gratefully accepted a cup of coffee offered by a trooper next to a bravely flickering campfire. Nothing in urban life matches the taste of coffee boiled in a covered pan over a campfire. *And if anything did*, Rep thought as he choked the stuff down, *it would be a Class B misdemeanor to sell it.*

He made his way toward the target range and the modern conveniences that Peter had said lay beyond it. He glanced in the general direction of Jackrabbit Press, shaking his head at the remnants of a dark gray ash-cloud that hung languidly in the air over an outbuilding chimney. *Who would have had an indoor fire last night in this heat?* he wondered.

As he walked through the pale, post-dawn light, he realized with some surprise that he didn't really have any enthusiasm for the legal project Lawrence had dangled in front of him. He didn't want Lawrence's shiny, spiffed up, video-game, Power Ranger Union soldiers wandering around a camp like this in their custom-designed, operetta-pretty, combed cotton uniforms. He didn't want Lawrence to sell a few more bodice-rippers by co-opting the reverence to memory and history that the re-enactors were offering here. He didn't blame Lawrence, who had a mass-market business to run. But Rep couldn't generate much excitement about contributing to it. It would be like helping someone use a classic rock anthem to sell laxatives. *No, wait a minute,* Rep thought, *I DID that. This would be worse.*

Rep's pace quickened as he came within sight of his objective.

"Looks like we're headed for the same place."

Startled, Rep glanced over at the man who'd come out of nowhere to fall in beside him. Jedidiah Whatsisname—Trevelyan, the sutler whose sharp practice with a widow had won him an antique Barlow knife and an enemy.

"Good morning," Rep said.

"Mornin'. Mind those roots. Hard to see in this light, an' they'll just reach out an' grab you."

Rep snapped his head to look down, and in the next instant felt himself sailing inelegantly through the air. As he completed a pratfall on mud and sodden grass, he felt the sutler falling beside and on top of him.

"Whoa, hoss, that's one now!" Trevelyan said, already scrambling to his knees. "Here, let's get you up an' brushed off."

In his startled confusion, Rep had the bizarre notion for a split second that the man had designs on stealing his saber. He clamped both hands clumsily to it. Then, back on his feet, he came to his senses as clumps of mud gave way to Trevelyan's vigorous hand swipes.

"There. Good as new."

"Thanks," Rep said. "I don't know how that happened."

"Walkin' around outside before full light is something you have to get used to, that's all," Trevelyan said. "Which stall you favor?"

Rep chose the nearest of the five Port-A-Potties available. With a couple of tugs he worked the balky door open and started to step inside. He stepped back fast. Very fast.

R. Thomas Quinlan—as he would later be identified to Rep—sat hunched on the toilet. His chin was much too low, and drenching his upper torso was a still viscous liquid that looked dark brown but glinted damply with hints enough of bright red to stamp it unmistakably as blood.

"Whoa, hoss," Trevelyan said with a long, low whistle. "Whatcha got there? Yankee woke up with his hat in his lap, eh? Not the first time that ever happened around these parts, but even so."

"Okay," Rep stammered, telling himself to get a grip. "Okay. Um, look. Uh, first, please don't say, 'Whoa, hoss,' again for a few minutes, okay? And second, we need a cop, and we need one in a hurry."

"You don't watch where you're pointin' you're gonna piss on one," a booming voice responded from ten feet away.

Rep's preparations hadn't actually advanced nearly so far, but the hyperbolic comment got his attention. The source of the voice was taller than Lawrence and broader through the chest than Trevelyan was through the belly, which was saying something. His butternut gray slouch hat contrasted with a bushy, rust-colored beard and heroic sideburns. He wore red-trimmed gray trousers and suspenders over a long-sleeved, off-white undershirt. If he worried about treacherous roots reaching out and grabbing his feet as he strode forward, his confident gait didn't show it.

"Good morning, Jedidiah," the new arrival said after he had closed the distance, which didn't take long. "Got yourself some fresh meat here?"

"Now it's not like that, Red, there's a body—"

"I saw that trip," Red commented. He turned an appraising eye in Rep's direction. Then, swinging his gaze back to Trevelyan, he held out his hand.

"Red," Trevelyan protested, "I'm tellin' you there's a body—"

"Last chance," Red said.

"Oh!" Trevelyan said. "You mean this young feller's button that came off in the fall and that I found while I was helping him up. Here it is. I was just about to give it back to him."

Trevelyan unfolded his right hand and dropped a dull, tarnished metal button perhaps a half-inch in diameter into Red's palm. Red immediately offered it to Rep.

"I believe this is your property, sir," he said.

Rep accepted the trinket with his left hand while with his right he felt the empty space on his shell jacket where it belonged.

"Thanks very much," he said. "This uniform belongs to somebody else, and I'd like to give it back to him intact."

"You know," Red said, "during the War for Southern Independence soldiers with sticky fingers could get bucked and gagged. Tied in a sitting position with a stick holding their elbows under their knees. Leave 'em that way for twelve hours or so. Sutlers, though, they just horsewhipped."

"Now, Red," Trevelyan whined, "I told you already—"

"You mean he went through that whole thing to steal a button?" Rep asked. "Tracked me down, managed to run into me, tripped me? I saw buttons like this at the sutlers' tent being sold for a quarter apiece."

"You saw replicas," Red said. "I'm betting that what you're holding there is the thing itself, actually worn by a pony soldier during the late, lamented Struggle. Maybe rode with Little Phil Sheridan himself, for all we know. Collector might pay three-hundred fifty dollars for it."

Rep remembered Trevelyan's searching, close-up inspection the day before, while he was ostensibly touting the virtues of different revolvers to Rep.

"Now, dammit, I'm not gonna stand here and have my good name blackened," Trevelyan said. "I'm gonna—"

"I'll tell you what you're gonna do, and right fast," Red said. "You're gonna hop over to the Confederate side of the encampment. You're gonna say that Sergeant Pendleton of the Missouri Partisan Rangers would be much obliged if a buncha boys from the General Order Number 11 Club would hot-foot it over here. And if I see twelve of them within fifteen minutes, I might pretend to swallow that hogswill you've been peddling ever since I got here."

Trevelyan made tracks without further commentary. *Who would have imagined he could move so fast?* Rep thought.

"So it's Sergeant Red Pendleton," Rep said. "I'm Private Rep Pennyworth. I'm new at this."

"We were all new at it once. Anyhoo, I'm now gonna start acting like a sergeant in the Missouri Highway Patrol, which I also happen to be, 'cause I don't think that fella in the can there died of natural causes. Don't tell anybody about this. It's against the rules, but duty is duty."

Pendleton pulled a cell phone from his trouser pocket as he carefully stepped away from the Port-A-Potty, gesturing to Rep to follow him. With an emphatic sweeping motion of his left arm, he waved three approaching re-enactors away from the area.

"Hey, Smitty, that you?" he said into the phone. "This is Red Pendleton. Listen, we got ourselves a homicide up at the Civil War encampment south of Liberty, down by the johns.…This is Clay County, but I'm betting the closest CSI van is probably the Jackson County Sheriff's Department.…Yeah, call Jackson County, tell them maybe it's a Metro Squad thing, get that van up here. We need to get that baby to work, 'cause it's gonna take a miracle to keep this crime scene secure for more than half an hour."

He put the phone away, took his hat off, and swiped his right sleeve across his forehead.

"You know who that fella is?" he asked Rep, nodding toward the body.

"No," Rep said. He'd never met Quinlan, or heard him described.

"Quite a blade you've got there."

"I bought it yesterday," Rep said.

"Mind if I take a look at it?" Pendleton asked.

"Actually," Rep said, "I'm inclined to insist on it." He started to reach for a handkerchief, but Pendleton waved that nicety aside.

"We know your fingerprints are on there, and no one's gonna try to pin this on me," he said.

Rep unhooked the scabbard and tendered the saber hilt-first to Pendleton. Pendleton drew the weapon, examined the blade for perhaps a minute, then passed it under his nose an inch at a time and sniffed deeply.

"Well," he said, "they'll wanna do a spectrographic analysis because you were the one that found the body, but I'll guarantee you there hasn't been any blood or human tissue on that blade in the last twenty-four hours."

"That's a relief."

"Lemme just try somethin' before I give this back to you. Throw one of those twigs up in the air, would ya?"

Rep complied, tossing up a stick about two feet long. Pendleton slashed with the saber, which knocked the stick several feet but didn't sever it. Rep retrieved the twig and showed Pendleton a gash perhaps a quarter-inch deep in the surface.

"On a good day," Pendleton said after examining it, "this saber of yours could just about cut hot butter."

"I hadn't even thought of sharpening it."

"Don't think about it. At re-enactments we want the metal to clang so the tourists get a show, but we don't actually wanna slice anybody up. If there's a saber out here that could do the kinda cuttin' our quiet friend over there experienced, somebody had to take some extra effort with it."

The sound of hurrying feet drew Rep's attention to a stand of trees off to his left. Nine men in gray came out on the double, carrying muskets.

"Morning, Sergeant," the one in front called. "What's the drill?"

"Morning," Pendleton bawled. "It would oblige me if you would form a perimeter around these fancy latrines here. Gimme twelve paces if you can."

After a brief look of puzzlement, the guy in front snapped a salute—a pretty good salute, too, if Rep was any judge—and hustled off with his buddies to comply.

"So," Rep said as he took his saber back, "what do we do now?"

"We wait," Pendleton said. "And hope someone brings us breakfast."

Chapter 11

"Here's your toothpick back, Yank, and a souvenir for your trouble."

Rep took the saber that Pendleton handed to him, along with a strip of paper not quite three inches wide and eight inches long. Two columns of letters and numbers ran down the strip. The numbers on the left seemed a lot different than the numbers on the right.

"There doesn't seem to be a drop of sweat, a dab of blood, or a smidgeon of deoxyribonucleic acid in the deceased's body that matches up with anything on that saber," Pendleton said. "He apparently never even breathed on it, much less got his throat slit and his head damn near cut off with it."

"Not a surprise," Rep said, "but it's nice to have it confirmed."

Pendleton dropped to the ground and lounged beside Rep, propping himself up on one elbow. Rep still didn't have a watch but Pendleton did—a large, stem-wound pocket watch that Henry Clay might have used—and he reported that it was just past nine in the morning. They were lying about fifty feet from the crime scene, which was now surrounded by yellow tape and swarming with deputy sheriffs from two counties and detectives from the Kansas City Police Department.

"First thing you think about with a guy his age killed out in the middle of nowhere like this is some kind of drug deal gone sour," Pendleton mused.

"You have a lot of drug dealers running around northwest Missouri with machetes or cutlasses?" Rep asked.

"Nope, and that's a fact," Pendleton said. "Uzis and up for them. Don't kid yourself, though. Plenty of those boys favor knives for detail work, and a Buck skinning knife with a five-inch blade could've done the job our stiff got done on him. You wouldn't need a saber for it."

Rep nodded politely but didn't comment.

"They oughta have your statement printed out before too much longer. Sorry about all this waitin' around, but there's nothin' for it when you're the one stumbles over a body."

"That's okay," Rep said. "You can learn things while you're waiting, if you pay attention."

"That a fact?" Pendleton asked jovially. "You learned anything so far?"

"Well," Rep said lazily, "I learned that pan-fried sausage patties in between slices of cornbread steeped in bacon grease makes a breakfast that sticks with you for a long time. I appreciate you having some of your boys bring that up, by the way."

"That's an interesting thing," Pendleton said. "How some foods that you generally eat hot actually taste better cold. Bacon, for one example. You almost always eat bacon warm off the griddle, but bacon at room temperature or even with a little chill on it—man, that's meat for me. Nothin' like it."

"I'd never really thought about it, but you're absolutely right," Rep said. "Steak is that way. Sizzling hot it's great, but if you save a little chunk, wrap it in wax paper and aluminum foil, put it in the refrigerator overnight, then pull it out the next morning when you're wife isn't looking, sprinkle a little salt on it and eat it like finger food—man, that's good."

"Yessir!" Pendleton said with an enthusiasm bordering on passion. "I can almost taste it right now. And how about fried chicken?"

"Oh, yeah," Rep said with a vigorous nod. "Not in aluminum foil, though. In a sandwich bag, two pieces per bag. Especially wings and thighs, pan fried and then in the fridge maybe, what, thirty-six hours."

"My word, my word, you are onto something there, my friend. I could jaw about this all morning. It doesn't work for everything. Eggs have to be hot, and hot dogs. But a lot of main course food out there is best eaten cold."

Like revenge, Rep thought. *According to Francis Bacon, a dish best tasted cold. As opposed to the way revenge had been tasted when the corpse here launched his bark on the dark seas of eternity last night.* Rep suspected that Pendleton's literary allusion was perfectly deliberate, and he readily deciphered the hint. Pendleton wasn't a hayseed, despite the act. He wasn't buying his own eyewash about a drug deal, and he wanted Rep to know it.

Rep had also learned some other things in the past few hours. He had learned that, like so many things in life, relieving yourself in the woods without benefit of a privy is only hard the first time you do it. More important, he had learned that the murder victim was named R. Thomas Quinlan and had had some kind of connection with Jackrabbit Press. Rep hadn't exactly been chatty before learning that, but he'd gotten downright laconic since. Now he was learning that Pendleton thought he knew something about this murder that he hadn't mentioned yet. Rep suspected that this might be so, but he was going to go on not mentioning it until he'd talked to Melissa. And to Peter.

"What's General Order Number 11?" he asked Pendleton, pulling himself to a sitting position as he saw a plainclothes officer in shirtsleeves approaching him with a notebook.

"'All persons living in Jackson, Cass and Bates Counties, Missouri…are hereby ordered to remove from their present places of residence within fifteen days…. [A]ll grain and hay found in such district after the ninth of September next…will be destroyed.'"

"Pretty drastic."

"Do you remember a movie from the Eighties, I think it was, called *The Outlaw Josey Wales*?" Pendleton asked.

"Sure. Clint Eastwood. Shows up on TBS all the time."

"The first bad guy in that flick is a Union general nicknamed Redlegs. That was General Thomas Ewing, and General Order Number 11 was his handiwork. Missouri had stayed in the Union, but the idea wasn't exactly unanimous. Lots of secessionist guerrilla activity. General Order Number 11 was supposed to stop it, and if a few thousand civilians got in the way that was just too bad for them. George Caleb Bingham made a famous painting about families being uprooted and homes abandoned. My grandmother kept a print of that painting in her front hallway until the day she died. She'd heard stories from her grandma about the day the Yankees burned the crop, and when she told me those stories it was like it happened the day before yesterday."

"Desperate times, I guess," Rep said, resorting to banality to mask his interest in the answer. *Was Lawrence a closet Confederate sympathizer? Did the framed document he'd seen in Lawrence's study suggest some pathological obsession with the Lost Cause?*

Rep and Pendleton rose to greet the detective, who handed Rep a three-ring binder he was carrying.

"This is the statement we took from you earlier, sir," the man said, all business. "Please read it carefully, initial each page, sign the last page, and return it to me. The copy is for you. If you wish to make any changes, please consult with me before altering the document."

"Certainly," Rep said. *I have a feeling that's not the first time he's ever made that speech*, he thought. Thought, but didn't say. He read, initialed, and signed as instructed and returned the binder to the detective.

"Thank you for your cooperation, sir. Please contact the department before leaving the state."

"Wound pretty tight, isn't he?" Rep commented to Pendleton after the detective had marched away.

"Oh, you send one of those city boys to Quantico for baby detective school and he comes back thinkin' he has a square asshole. He thought it was high-handed for me to bring a county crime scene team in here. If I hadn't, though, you'd have waited 'til noon to sign that statement."

"Much obliged," Rep said.

"What's on your mind, soldier?" Pendleton bellowed then over his shoulder.

Startled, Rep looked around. A Union private was standing about ten feet away, apparently hanging back.

"I have a message for Trooper Pennyworth," the man said.

"Well if he's a trooper he'd be the one with boots instead of brogans," Pendleton said.

The man advanced and handed Rep a folded slip of paper. *Need to see you ASAP. I'm with the car at Jackrabbit Press. M*

"Orders," Rep said to Pendleton as he sketched a casual salute. "I'll be in touch."

"Oh, I expect you will at that," Pendleton said as Rep strode away. "I expect you will."

Chapter 12

"In the eight years we've been married, Melissa, how many times have I put my foot down?"

"Twice." Melissa glanced demurely downward before raising her eyes earnestly to meet her husband's. "You were quite thrilling on both occasions."

"Well, time for the hat trick. We're talking about a homicide. That saber on the chair over there could be a murder weapon."

"Yes, dear, I do grasp that."

They were standing in the Damons' bedroom just before ten thirty in the morning. During the drive from the encampment, as mile after mile of Kansas City pavement had slipped under their wheels, Melissa had told Rep about the Problem. With Peter's disappearance, the Problem had had a capital P even when it was just a regrettable, one-time slipping of the marital traces—that is, even before Rep mentioned the corpse.

"Linda and I got back to their home around eleven thirty last night," Melissa had explained as they drove through the Plaza. "We found Peter's uniform but not Peter. Linda went out checking some all-night haunts while I called a few friends she told me about. Nada. No answer at his work number or on his cell phone. We were out of ideas when she got back around three, so we decided to stay there and wait for him to show up."

"Sounds like the right move," Rep had commented.

"Except that by eight thirty this morning, Peter still hadn't come home. No contact, no messages. Linda was frantic, and I wasn't feeling so great myself. So she went out looking for him while I drove to the encampment to see if he'd gone back there. That's when I asked someone to track you down."

"So I'm up to date," Rep had said.

"Right. Peter's disappearing act would be troubling under any circumstances, but coming so soon after Linda let R. Thomas Quinlan talk her into the sack on a vulnerable night it's hard not to get shook about it."

"*WHAT?* The guy she slept with was Quinlan?"

These emphatic questions, fortunately, had come while they were stopped at a red light just before turning onto the south-bound leg of Ward Parkway.

"Yes. I forgot, you've never met him. He has his own imprint at Jackrabbit Press, and Linda works with him a lot."

"'*Had* his own imprint,'" Rep had said. "Last night, R. Thomas Quinlan passed away. Passed away, as it happens, courtesy of a very sharp blade *after* Peter retrieved his saber and said he had something to take care of."

"That was what all the excitement at the encampment was about?"

"Yes."

"This just got vastly worse, didn't it?"

"And it's headed downhill from there," Rep had said. "I was the one who found the body. So you might say that I have met Quinlan, although I suppose that raises a metaphysical issue."

They had gone into the Damons' house hoping that Linda, at least, would have returned. But they had found the house empty. Their search had ended in the bedroom, where Melissa had started hinting about Rep giving Peter some legal help and Rep had put his foot down.

"We can hold their hands and be here for them and find out who the best criminal lawyer in Kansas City is if it turns out Peter needs one," Rep said after Melissa shrugged off his initial demurrer. "But I can't play Ben Matlock. In this little mess I'm not a lawyer, I'm a witness. And so are you."

"I'm duly admonished," Melissa said. "But you don't seriously believe that Peter killed Quinlan, do you?"

"I don't know. But I know that heavy cavalry sabers have long, substantial blades. And I'll feel much better if the cops don't find any blood on Peter's when they examine it."

"Now there's an interesting point," Melissa said brightly.

Darting around her husband, she crossed to the woven wicker chair where Peter had apparently thrown his uniform and equipment (other than his bugle) sometime late last night. She pulled on the white gauntlets lying there, picked up the saber, and awkwardly slipped the weapon from its scabbard.

"I suppose it's pointless for me to note that you're tampering with evidence," Rep said resignedly, but he made no effort to stop her. He wanted to know the answer as much as she did.

"I'm doing my level best *not* to tamper with it," Melissa answered.

They examined the blade together. Rep pointed to a few specks of dark discoloration about two-thirds of the way down.

"It looks too brown for blood," Melissa said.

"Thank you, Doctor Quincy."

"And if Peter had cut a man's throat you'd think there'd be a lot more."

"I don't know what color dried blood is, and I don't know if those specks are what's left after a lot more blood was wiped off. But I'm surprised to see any at all. I would have expected Peter to keep this thing in mint condition."

Pulling his own gauntlets on, Rep worked a loose, broken wicker strut free from the chair back. He extended his right hand toward Melissa, who with some reluctance turned the saber over to him. Rep tossed the wicker into the air and slashed theatrically at it with the saber. Unfortunately, he missed, which somewhat diluted his gesture's dramatic impact. He tried again and this time made contact. The saber sliced cleanly through half an inch of wood.

"Very impressive, dear, but isn't that what sabers are supposed to do?"

"Mine didn't. These things are supposed to be props. Reenactments aren't intended to spill real blood."

Melissa realized that what she was about to do was manipulative, and reminded herself to feel ashamed later on. Her face formed an exasperated pout, which she turned away from Rep as soon as she was sure he'd seen it.

"You're upset with my dogmatic, left-brained, patriarchal, stereotypically male logical empiricism, right?" Rep asked.

"Let's just say that if I gave you a swat right now it would be aggravation, not flirtation," Melissa said. "Which wouldn't be fair, because you're right. Logically, things don't look particularly good."

"Well, it's not *all* one way," Rep allowed. "There's no blood on the uniform, which should have gotten thoroughly spattered from the kind of attack that killed Quinlan. Peter certainly didn't seem coldly homicidal when he was retrieving his saber and talking to me. And with a guy like Quinlan seems to have been, there are probably several cuckolded husbands in the Kansas City metropolitan area who would have been happy to cut his throat."

"Go on," Melissa said, her face glowing with ostensible admiration for her husband's rhetorical brilliance. "You're certainly convincing me."

With a mordant smile at his wife, Rep took the scabbard from her and decisively re-sheathed the saber.

"You don't really think I'm swallowing that little routine, do you, Doctor Pennyworth?" he asked then.

"Uh oh," Melissa said. "I rather thought you were, actually."

"Listen," he said tenderly, putting the saber back on the chair. "I know how much Linda means to you. I know you feel that Linda confiding in you and you giving her advice means you have a special responsibility."

"But," Melissa prompted.

"But Peter had a sharp piece of metal there when someone he had a motive to kill got killed with a sharp piece of metal. You're resisting the obvious. With anyone else I'd say emotional involvement got in the way of objectivity. But you're too smart for me to blow your argument off like that."

"Rep, dearest, " Melissa said, "I know exactly what you're up to."

"So I want you to do something," Rep continued. "Think about it for a minute, and then tell me how much of your attitude is coming from your heart and how much is coming from your head."

"You're not playing fair," Melissa said.

"That doesn't exactly set a precedent in this conversation, does it?"

"Okay." Melissa took a deep breath. She closed her eyes. She forced herself to think methodically for sixty seconds. "Okay," she said again. "Time for a little dose of G. K. Chesterton."

"Dose away."

"Suppose an eleven-year-old girl told you that she'd seen a vision of the Blessed Virgin or Mother Teresa. Would you believe her?"

"No," Rep said.

"Neither would I. But would you be absolutely certain?"

Rep opened his mouth for a hip-shot answer, then stopped and thought for a few seconds.

"This will sound like a cop-out," he said, "but I don't think I could say I was 'absolutely certain' about anything. Things happen that we don't understand. Fatima, Lourdes. The time-space continuum bending in on itself. 'Absolutely certain?' I guess not."

"Now, suppose someone told you that he was sitting in the bleachers on the Capitol steps last inauguration day and he saw Laura Bush smoking a cigar while her husband was being sworn in. Would you believe him?"

"No, of course not."

"Neither would I," Melissa said. "Would you be absolutely certain he was wrong?"

"That's a trick question," Rep protested.

"Why?"

"Well, it's not the same thing. I mean, yeah, I would be as close to absolutely certain as you could be. It's not the kind of thing that would happen at all, much less happen and be ignored by everyone who had to have seen it except one guy."

"Right," Melissa said. "It wouldn't violate any scientific laws, the way a miraculous vision would. But it would violate the laws of human nature."

"So what are you saying? That Peter Damon couldn't have killed a man who seduced his wife?"

"No. I'm not even sure I could say that about you—not that I expect the question ever to come up."

"So who's Laura Bush in this analogy, and what's the cigar?"

"Peter didn't have a breath of a motive unless he at least suspected that Linda had cheated on him with Quinlan."

"How do we know he didn't suspect that?" Rep demanded. "All we know is that Linda didn't tell him about the fling. He could have spotted Quinlan's little keepsake and parsed it the same way you did."

"If he had suspected infidelity on any grounds, he wouldn't have gone running off while his wife was in the bathroom, maybe overdosing on something in a paroxysm of remorse. Anyone can see how desperately he loves her. He might have screamed at her or—or any number of things, I suppose. But he apodictically would not have left Jackrabbit Press until he saw with his own eyes that she was physically okay."

"If you're right, then when Peter came down to get his saber he didn't even suspect Linda had cheated, much less that Quinlan was the guy, and therefore he couldn't have been planning to kill him. Wait a minute, though. What if he'd noticed the hairs tied to the bolt but didn't tumble to what it meant until he was five miles down the road?"

"And then doubled back to kill Quinlan?" Melissa asked.

"Right."

"The timing doesn't work. Linda and I were only about twenty minutes behind him. If he'd driven off and then back-tracked to kill Quinlan, he couldn't have gotten home, changed clothes, and left before Linda and I got there."

"Fair enough," Rep said. "Which takes us back to the key question: if it wasn't jealous rage that sent Peter running off in the first place, what was it? If we can answer that question *and* sell your laws-of-human-nature premise, then what Peter said to me not only isn't incriminating, it's almost an alibi."

"But the police don't sleep with me, so they won't pay any attention to metaphysical speculation borrowed from G. K. Chesterton. Once they get a sharp saber and a whiff of adultery, they'll stop looking at anything else and work on nailing Peter for the murder. He needs help from someone else."

"Which unfortunately can't be us," Rep said. "Apart from everything else, there's the detail that I don't know any criminal law. I deliberately forgot everything I'd learned about it fifteen minutes after the bar exam."

"Well," Melissa said dubiously, "nobody's perfect."

"Although you come close, beloved. But close doesn't cut it. We can't pull a Nick-and-Nora here."

"That verged on condescending."

"It was a literary allusion," Rep protested.

"I guess it was, at that. I suppose I should be flattered."

The phone rang. They both sprang to answer it. This involved a mild collision, a moment's confusion, and a rare unladylike ejaculation from Melissa, for the Damons' bedroom phone was cunningly concealed somewhere with its ringer turned off, and Rep and Melissa had instinctively headed first for the telephone locations in their own home. Rep managed to find the Damons' phone in the living room by the fourth ring, as Melissa picked up the kitchen extension.

"Damon residence, Rep Pennyworth speaking," Rep said.

"This isn't Peter?" a male voice that Rep didn't quite recognize asked.

"No, my wife and I are guests of the Damons. Peter isn't here right now."

"How about Linda?"

"Not at the moment, I'm afraid. Can I take a message?"

"Yes. In fact, it's lucky you answered. This is John Paul Lawrence."

"Yes, of course. I'm terribly sorry about Mr. Quinlan's death. That must be a terrible blow both to you and your company."

"That is exactly right, and you're very kind to say so. I was hoping to reach Linda to talk both about a fitting memorial for Tom, and somewhat less sentimentally about keeping his projects on track."

"I'll have her call you as soon as I see her," Rep said.

"Ordinarily, I would have put that call off at least until tomorrow. But I heard a few minutes ago that the detectives investigating Tom's murder have been told that Linda was seen last night talking with him, even though he hadn't planned on coming to the social."

"I see," Rep said.

"Andy Pignatano is a local lawyer who does criminal work and is highly regarded. He is coming out here at two thirty. I thought it might be a good idea for Linda to join us in a consultation. You as well, for that matter."

"I'll try to get word to her, and if I can get out there myself I will."

"Good. Hope to see you then."

Phones clicked. When Melissa returned to the living room, she saw Rep hurriedly unbuttoning his shell jacket while he hustled toward the stairs.

"See if you can find a large cardboard box," he yelled over his shoulder, panting because he was taking two steps at a time. "Hurry!"

Cardboard box? she wondered.

"No, wait, that's dumb," Rep said, pausing breathlessly at the top of the stairs and unbuckling his belt. "Boot my computer up and plug in the phone modem. First, send an e-mail to the all-attorneys list at the firm asking for recommendations of the top three criminal lawyers in Kansas City. Then get on the net and search for TASA."

"T-A-S-A?" Melissa asked, as if she were involved in a sane conversation. "And what's wrong with the Pignatano guy?"

"To answer your questions in order," Rep yelled from the bedroom, "yes, and nothing as far as I know, except that I don't know whose lawyer he is."

Rep stripped off his uniform and equipment and tossed them on the bed. He climbed gratefully back into the twenty-first century clothes he'd left in this room less than twenty-four hours before. Then he turned to the Damons' closets. He started to pick up a suitcase, checked himself, and chose a large suit carrier instead. He laid this on the bed.

"Honey," Melissa called to him, "I've sent the e-mail, and I've gotten three hundred fifty-two catches on TASA. Which one do I want?"

"Technical Advisory Services for Attorneys," he yelled in response.

He found the calico dresses that Linda and Melissa had presumably worn last night and slid them into the suit carrier. Then he stuffed Peter's uniform and saber into the bag on top of the dresses.

"I have Technical Advisory and so forth," Melissa yelled. "What next?"

"Look for 'chemical analysts' or something like that," Rep shouted.

He zipped the suit carrier shut. Now came the part that was tickling his conscience a little bit. *Well,* he thought, *might as well be hanged for a sheep as a lamb.* He took his own uniform and saber and arrayed them on the wicker chair where Peter's had been.

"How about forensic chemists?" Melissa bellowed.

"Perfect," Rep screeched. "See if there's one in Kansas City."

"I didn't think you wanted one in Tampa, luv," Melissa said with exaggerated patience. "Done."

"Good." Rep spoke this syllable as he was walking down the stairs, lugging the garment bag over his shoulder. "Get the address and phone number down while I put this in the car."

"I'm printing it out now. I thought we weren't doing Nick and Nora."

"Well, we're sure not going to sit around here and wait for the Kansas City Police Department to show up with a search warrant."

"Is this sudden change because of what Lawrence said about someone seeing Linda talking to Quinlan?"

"Yes. Because maybe that's what someone saw, and maybe what someone saw was a young woman in a long calico dress talking to Quinlan."

"Namely me."

"Namely you."

"I'm already getting some answers to the e-mails."

"Print out as many as you can in two minutes," Rep said, heading for the kitchen where the back door was, "then come to the car. And leave the front door unlocked so that the cops won't have to break it down."

Having learned a share of patience in eight years of marriage, Rep waited almost six minutes in the car. Then, sighing, he went back in the house to see what was holding Melissa up. He found her talking on the phone.

"It's Linda," she said.

"Any sign of Peter yet?"

"No."

Rep went into the living room and picked up the phone there.

"Linda, this is Rep. Where are you now?"

"At the library. No one here has seen Peter, but he signed in at the guard station around midnight, and signed out again at twelve forty-eight."

Twelve forty-EIGHT? Rep thought. *How anal is THAT?*

"Okay. Listen, Linda, don't come home yet. Check into a hotel under your own name. Call Melissa's cell phone and just say the name of the hotel."

"What's going on?" Linda demanded.

"We'll talk later. Just do as I ask, okay?"

"Okay. I guess. Rep, Melissa, I'm really worried about Peter."

"That's all right. We'll talk soon."

"All right."

Melissa met Rep at the back door.

"'Check into a hotel under your own name'?" she asked. "I thought you didn't remember anything from your criminal law course."

"I don't. I learned that by watching Perry Mason reruns."

Chapter 13

For what this guy's probably going to charge, Melissa thought, *I would have expected at least a lab coat.*

Wesley Cerv, Ph.D. and CEO of Litigation Analysts, Inc., had his offices not in Kansas City but in suburban Shawnee Mission, on the Kansas side of the line. He greeted them in blue jeans and a tee-shirt showing a bronze bust of a moon-faced man, accompanied by the words

Major League Record
Home Runs in a Non-Expansion Season
Without Chemical Assistance
George Herman (Babe) Ruth—60 (1927)

"I agree with the sentiment," Rep said. "Although I think that, technically, alcohol may qualify as a chemical."

"Not performance enhancing, however," Cerv said. "By the way, my retainer is twenty-five hundred dollars."

"Let's see if you want the case first," Rep said. Opening the suit carrier, he displayed the contents for Cerv and explained that they wanted to know about any matches between trace elements on these items and the Quinlan DNA results on the printout Pendleton had given Rep.

"Would this have anything to do with that murder out at the Civil War encampment that they're talking about on the radio?"

"That's what I'm hoping you can tell me," Rep said.

"You understand that I'm not one of those experts who asks you the chemist's equivalent of how much you want two and two to be—right?"

"I certainly hope not," Rep said.

"If any of this stuff turns out to be possible evidence in a murder case, I can't sit on it. It would have to go to the police as soon as I had hard data."

"Of course. How long will it take to get hard data?"

"That depends," Cerv said, steepling his fingers thoughtfully. "How long do you want it to take?"

"About two days."

"Not three months? So your guy might be innocent, huh?"

"Let's hope we know in two days," Rep said.

"I take American Express," Cerv said.

Ten minutes later Melissa was steering the Taurus off of State Line Road onto Sixty-Third Street, on the way back to Ward Parkway.

"So," she said. "I think checking the library again for traces of Peter and maybe chatting with Chelsea Tuttle if I can arrange to run into her stops well short of playing Nick and Nora. Any other ideas about how to pass the time while we wait for Cerv's report?"

"Try to get Peter and Linda a lawyer," Rep shrugged. "Meet Pignatano. Hook up with Linda when she calls. Nose around the encampment."

"Nose around the encampment about what?"

"Peter. And whether Jedidiah Trevelyan is an even bigger crook than Sergeant Pendleton thinks he is."

"Let a man once stoop to button thieving and he will not stick at murder," Melissa said. "I'll bet Ben Jonson would have said that if he'd thought of it."

"It sounds thin," Rep sighed, "and Chelsea Tuttle murdering her editor as a negotiating tactic doesn't seem like a betting proposition either. But maybe the framed document and the medal on Lawrence's wall mean that he's into Civil War collectibles. Maybe Trevelyan sold him some that were stolen or inauthentic. Maybe Quinlan found out."

Correctly interpreting Melissa's polite silence as skeptical, Rep started calling criminal lawyers. He had to call all three numbers Melissa had printed out before he reached an attorney who was neither in court nor in conference. Norm Archer said he was pleased to have been recommended, and asked Rep what he could do for him.

"Not sure yet. You free tomorrow?"

"Wide open."

"Let's shoot for nine-thirty," Rep said. "I'll check with the potential client and call you back if we can't make it. Meanwhile, what can you tell me about Andy Pignatano?"

"If it's an immigration problem or a white collar rap, Andy's your guy. Medicaid fraud, commercial bribery, visa extension, embezzlement, borrowing money on collateral that doesn't exist—he's the man."

"How about murder?" Rep asked.

"The next murder case Andy wins will be the first one," Archer said. "He likes to associate with a more intellectual class of criminal."

"Thanks. Talk to you later."

Glancing at his cell phone as he ended the call, Rep noticed that he had messages waiting. Which figured. He'd left the phone at the Damons when he and Peter went to the encampment. He was about to start checking them when Melissa's phone beeped. She nodded at Rep, for she belonged to the shut-up-and-drive school. Rep switched phones and answered.

"Rep?" Linda's voice.

"Yeah."

"Okay. Doubletree at Thirteenth and Wyandotte."

"We're on our way," Rep said. He relayed the information to Melissa.

"The more I think about Quinlan having his own imprint the more it bothers me," she said as she turned onto the Southwest Trafficway. "An imprint is a kind of consecration, a statement to the trade that you're a master craftsman—the kind of editor who'd spend four hours getting a single sentence exactly right. Quinlan struck me as a shallow schmoozer with a gift of gab. I can't see him spending four hours on an entire chapter—especially if he had a hot date scheduled."

"Well, you didn't exactly meet him in a professional context."

"I was at the place where he worked attending an event Jackrabbit Press was sponsoring, and for all he knew I was at the core of his target demographic. I would have felt better if he'd tried to dazzle me with Proust instead of pot. But it's not just that, there's also Linda's comments about him. 'That stuff about Titian and Giotto.... ' Cripes. I don't see how anyone as superficial and self-absorbed as he seemed could care passionately about how well other people write."

"Maybe giving him his own imprint was an ego thing—a substitute for paying him another twenty thousand a year," Rep said.

"Even without ego perks you don't need to pay DeLorean and Jamaican gold wages to get someone talented enough to do what Quinlan was doing," Melissa said as she pulled into a curving driveway in front of the Doubletree Hotel in downtown Kansas City. "Do you think you can find your way to the encampment from here?"

"If I get lost I'll call," Rep said.

A quick kiss and Melissa was gone. After a couple of hints from the doorman about getting to I-35 and then I-29 Rep pulled away from the hostelry. He waited until he had actually made it onto I-29 to retrieve the messages waiting for him on his cell phone. This was providential, for one of them, left at eight twelve that morning, would have distracted him from tasks far less intricate than finding a freeway entrance:

"Rep," a strangled voice said, "this is Peter. God, something terrible has happened. I have to talk to you. I don't know what to do. Oh, hell, you won't even get this message, and you can't reach me anyway. I'll try to get in touch with you, I guess."

Chapter 14

"I don't know where Quinlan was before you saw him drive up," Linda told Melissa around the time Rep hit I-35. "I didn't see him all night long."

The strains of "Lara's Theme" from *Doctor Zhivago* intervened. Melissa realized that this was the ring on Linda's cell phone. The soul of tact, she avoided rolling her eyes.

Linda leaped at the phone, her face simultaneously glowing with hope and twisted with anxiety. As she listened and spoke, she seemed to deflate.

"I see," Linda said. "No, I'm not sure what it's about. Maybe they're just checking everybody who was at the encampment. Thanks for calling."

"Police doing something?" Melissa asked as Linda ended the call.

"Yeah. That was Martha Herzog, one of our neighbors. She said two police cars came to our house, some cops went in, and they carried some clothing and other stuff out. Martha is, uh, kind of nosy."

"That doesn't come as a complete surprise," Melissa said. "Lawrence told Rep that someone claimed to have seen you talking to Quinlan last night. That's why my first question this morning was whether you'd seen him."

"But they couldn't have—Omigod! They saw you, didn't they, in that dress? Now I've gotten you mixed up in this mess."

"Stop it," Melissa said firmly. "I'm involved by my own choice. Rep found a lawyer who can see you tomorrow. That's up to you, but I vote yes. The question is, can we find Peter between now and then?"

"I'm out of ideas on that one."

"Rep thought you and I might nose around the library a bit."

"Long shot," Linda said. "Peter's boss, Diane Klimchock, accosted me there this morning. She said, 'Linda, has something got the wind up Peter? I have the oddest signal from him. It sounds like he's gone wobbly on me about testifying for the library expansion funding. We've had to delay our post to the committee.'"

"'Gone wobbly on me'? Linda, you're making that up."

"Swear to God," Linda said. "Imagine the president of the Charlotte Brontë Society on steroids, and you have Diane."

"Well, we're not going to accomplish anything here, so we might as well give it a try. Let's go."

The room phone rang. Melissa had already gotten to her feet, so she answered it and heard her husband's voice.

"I thought you were on your way to the encampment," she said.

"I am. I stopped at a gas station mini-mart to call you on a land line."

"What's up?"

"There was a message on my cell phone from Peter," Rep said. "When I called back the number he called from, I reached something called the Palm Gardens Hometel. No Peter Damon registered there. I got nothing from them over the phone, but maybe up close and personal would work better."

"Mini-mart?" Melissa asked suspiciously. "Rep, are you eating a Hostess Cream-Filled Cupcake?"

"Yes. I thought panfried sausage patties and cornbread might not be quite unhealthy enough to make me feel really macho."

"All right. Linda and I will check out the Palm Gardens Hometel."

The logical place for a local phone directory was the bedside table's top drawer, so what Melissa found there was, naturally, a Gideon Bible. She was rifling the second drawer when Linda came up with a phone book on the closet shelf.

"3699 Troost," Linda announced after paging rapidly through it.

The mild *frisson* that this address sent through Melissa and Linda marked them as Kansas City natives. The coasts stereotype KC as a placid bastion of Midwestern blandness and complacent middle class values. The city has always had a raffish facet to its personality, though, like an honor student sneaking a Marlboro on her way home from choir practice. Postwar reformers had tamed a Roaring Twenties/Depression-era legacy of genteel corruption, Mafia wars, and casual vice, but diluted vestiges of that rascality survived—and one of the places to find them in the comfortable city of leafy boulevards and bubbling fountains where Melissa and Linda had come of age was the midtown stretch of Troost.

In between the Missouri River on the north and ranch-house subdivisions hundreds of long blocks south, Troost runs past job shops, apartment buildings, shopping strips, martial arts schools, neighborhood bars, local drug stores, chain groceries, and working class residential areas. It separates the campuses of two universities, and borders churches from most Christian sects. But it also goes by fabled mob haunts, pornographic book stores, night spots featuring female impersonators, and the odd bordello. A 3699 address unambiguously evoked the seedier end of this gamut.

"Let's go," Melissa said briskly—briskly, because she was afraid that if she stopped to think about it she'd come up with a dozen very good reasons to check out the Jackson County Public Library instead.

"Coming," Linda said, sounding a lot braver than she looked.

A cab dropped them twelve minutes later under a plastic purple palm tree decorating the face of an aqua-colored overhang that shielded the main entrance of the Palm Gardens Hometel.

After Melissa had paid the fare, Linda nudged her and pointed to a tiny parking lot abutting the building. The Damons' lemon-yellow Volkswagen Beetle sat there forlornly, looking like it was afraid that PT Cruisers and Monte Carlos were about to break its glasses and steal its lunch money.

A raucous bell clanged as Linda and Melissa walked into the hotel. Without looking up from the issue of *Maxim* he was paging through, a desk clerk with a wispy, minuscule goatee said mechanically, "Forty-nine ninety-five a night, twelve dollars an hour."

"We're looking for someone," Melissa said as firmly as she could.

The desk clerk glanced up and frowned as he tried to focus on the women in the dim lobby light. He turned his head to be sure they could see his greasy rattail, which he apparently regarded as a tonsorial feature of considerable distinction.

"Good afternoon, ladies."

"I'm looking for my husband," Linda said as they reached the desk.

"Namely?"

"Peter Damon, but he apparently isn't registered under that name."

"That *will* happen," the man said.

"He made a phone call from here this morning," Melissa said.

"They *will* do that."

"His car is parked outside," Linda said. "He's just under six feet tall with light brown hair and kind of big ears. He would have come here sometime since midnight."

The man spread his arms and offered a smirk that said, *Are you kidding?*

Another man, taller than the desk clerk and with his more abundant but equally greasy black hair conventionally coiffed, came out from behind a partition in back of the desk.

"Moaner?" he asked the desk clerk.

"Could be," the desk clerk said.

"Local talent?" the man asked.

"These two?" the desk clerk demanded.

"No, you putz." The man punctuated this explanation with a jab at the desk clerk's bicep. "The one who checked out of the moaner's room."

"Her? No way."

"Come with me," the man said to Linda and Melissa, his tone suggesting that he could just barely stand talking to them. He whipped out from behind the desk and headed for a stairway toward the back of the lobby, with Linda and Melissa scurrying in his wake. They followed him to the second floor and then down a long corridor with turquoise doors and tapioca-colored walls to Room 226. He unlocked the door, opened it, and stood to one side.

"That him?" he asked.

"Peter!" Linda screamed. She pelted into the room and threw herself on the man twisted in the bedsheet—singular, for there was only one. His pants and underpants were bunched around his ankles, and his shirt was open.

"Clean him up and get him out of here," the man said, and stalked off.

Outside of horror movies, corpses don't groan or vomit. Peter was doing the first and had done the second quite recently, from the smell of things, so Melissa surmised that he wasn't dead. While Linda ministered to her suffering husband, Melissa looked around.

She could smell stale cigarette smoke, tinctured with something non-tobacco that she couldn't place. It wasn't pot—less sweet, with a little more tang. Two butts in an ashtray on the window sill had what looked like standard brown filters, but she couldn't see a brand. She picked up two styrofoam cups from the bedside table and sniffed them. They smelled faintly of orange juice. Her post-undergraduate experience with hard liquor consisted of five or six cocktails a year, but she thought she could have identified the whiff left by enough scotch or bourbon to coldcock Peter. Was it vodka that didn't have any odor? Maybe that was the answer, but she was dubious.

"He hardly drinks at all," Linda said, her voice shaking. "I don't know how he even choked down enough to get himself in this state."

"I don't think he's drunk," Melissa said.

"Then what happened to him?"

"I don't know." This struck Melissa as a more constructive answer than speculation about attempted suicide, and had the additional virtue of being true. "I'm calling an ambulance."

"St. Luke's is less than a mile away. Maybe we should just drive him to the emergency room."

"I'm not sure we could even get him down the stairs," Melissa said as she dialed nine-one-one. *And I'm not sure he has time for a couple of amateurs to try driving him a mile.*

A calm and reassuring voice answered Melissa's call. Following the voice's instructions, she identified herself and said where she was.

"And what is the problem?"

"A man here is near comatose, having some kind of a very bad physical reaction to something he ingested. Nausea, convulsions, loss of voluntary bodily functions, incoherence. Slipping in and out of consciousness."

"Drugs?" the voice asked.

"Don't know. I just got here." Melissa decided she'd have to punch the story up if she were going to make anything happen fast, so she began drawing on a smorgasbord of symptoms snatched willy-nilly from her broad exposure to mystery fiction. "Pulse rate is very low. Signs of shock. Lips turning blue. Eyeballs show white under his eyelids. We need an ambulance right away."

"Dispatching," the voice said.

Scarcely ten minutes later, Peter was strapped to a gurney on his way out of the Palm Gardens Hometel with Linda walking stricken beside him. Melissa had Linda's keys and Peter's shoes. She had given the two cups and, just for luck, the cigarette butts to one of the ambulance attendants.

"Can you take care of...things?" Linda asked over her shoulder.

"Of course. You stay with Peter. I'll get the car and find you at the hospital as soon as I can."

"Ah, excuse me, Miss, ah, excuse me," the desk clerk said to Melissa.

Melissa froze in place. The sound of the voice, all by itself, infuriated her. Her last real fist fight had been a two-punch affair in U-Twelve soccer more than twenty years before, but she was wondering if she had one good knuckle-busting swing left in her right arm.

"What is it?" she demanded.

"Well. Ah, technically, check-out time is twelve noon. So, ah, that would be another forty-nine ninety-five."

Not since a spasm of post-adolescent rebellion against respectability in her early twenties had Melissa used in its imperative mood the useful verb that English derives from the German *ficken*, meaning "to strike or to bang." She came very close to doing so now, but at the last second had a better idea.

"Let me see the room receipt," she snapped, striding over to the desk as if she had every right in the world to the document.

The desk clerk hesitated in an apparent agony of indecision, weighing the honor of the innkeepers' guild against the prospect of forty-nine dollars and ninety-five cents. Forty-nine ninety-five won. He thumbed through a tin box on the desk and produced a piece of paper.

Whoever checked in had identified herself as Anita Lay. She had written down a California address which Melissa memorized without any hope that it was genuine. She had signed in at six twelve yesterday evening. No credit-card information, vehicle data, or phone number.

"She paid cash?" Melissa asked.

"They *will* do that. Ah, do you think you could kinda step it up? You smell kinda funny. Are you nauseous?"

"No," Melissa said, graduate-assistant instincts triggered by the sloppy diction, "you're nauseous. I'm nauseated." She returned the receipt to him.

"Okay. What about the forty-nine ninety-five?"

Now Melissa used the verb.

Chapter 15

"Is it just my imagination, or are you missing one of the sabers you had displayed here yesterday afternoon?" Rep asked Trevelyan around one fifty.

This was a shot in the dark. It missed.

"Wish I was," Trevelyan said without hesitation, shaking his head. "When the cops picked my cutlery up for testing I said, 'Hell, you can keep 'em. I'm not doin' any good with 'em.' Haven't sold an edged weapon all week."

"How about that antique Barlow knife the young Confederate was so upset about yesterday?"

"If you're buyin', I believe I could find it. If you're teasin', I'm not in the mood. I bought that piece fair and square without lie-one in the bargain, and I don't care how upset that feller is, I mean to sell it at a handsome profit."

Rep mentally shrugged. Oh for two. Trevelyan now blinked as he suddenly seemed to remember Rep's face.

"You're outta uniform there, ain't ya, private? Where's your union suit?"

"At the tailor's," Rep said, "getting a button sewn on."

Trevelyan glanced down for a moment. When he spoke again, his voice had a little less rustic josh and a lot more shut-up-and-deal to it.

"Okay," he said. "What can I do for you?"

"Well, finding out that button was worth three hundred fifty dollars started me wondering about other Civil War collectibles."

"Anything in particular?"

"Start with medals. I don't know the name of the one I'm thinking about. I'm not even sure it's from the Civil War."

"The only two medals authorized in the United States armed forces during the Civil War were the purple heart and the congressional medal of honor," Trevelyan said. "The Rebs didn't have any atall."

Rep described as best he could the medal he'd seen displayed in Lawrence's office. Trevelyan shook his head.

"Not a Civil War medal, that's for sure," he said. "Doesn't sound like it's even American. Too fussy."

Rep's cell phone rang. He impatiently turned it off.

"How about documents?" he asked, carefully watching Trevelyan's face.

"Depends on the document."

"A copy of General Order Number 11," Rep said.

"General Ewing's?" Trevelyan asked.

Had to be a stall. How many other General Order Number 11's would Civil War hobbyists be interested in buying?

"Right," Rep said evenly. "General Ewing. Redlegs."

"Well," Trevelyan said, "copies of that order were supposed to go to every civilian in three counties, so a lot of them were printed up. Not all that rare. Genuine specimen, not too ratty, probably get ya twelve hundred. For ten percent I'll try to find someone who might be interested, or I'll take a look at what you got and tell you how much I'd take it off your hands for."

"You think someone like Mr. Lawrence might be interested in buying something like that?"

Trevelyan backed away from his side of the table and folded his arms across his chest, resting them on his ample belly.

"Here's the way it is, pilgrim," he said. "In this little deal you're talkin' about, you'd be bringin' a piece of paper with General Ewing's signature on it, and the buyer would be bringin' a check.

What I'd be bringin' is that I know the two of you and you don't know each other. So if I start tellin' you who buyers are, I don't have much left to sell except charm and good looks—and I'd starve to death peddlin' those."

"Actually, Mr. Lawrence already has a copy of General Order Number 11," Rep said. "Suppose I were interested in buying one, like he did. And suppose I wasn't too particular about where it came from or how it got here. You think you might be able to lay your hands on one?"

"You done got me a trifle confused," Trevelyan said. "One minute you maybe have one, and the next minute you maybe want one. When you git your mind made up what you're talkin' about, come back and we'll confabulate."

Rep noticed Trevelyan glance reflexively at a Navy Colt like the one he'd pitched to Rep yesterday. This one, though, wasn't in a display case. It was holstered, slung over the back of a chair a couple of feet from Trevelyan, and from what Rep could see of the cylinder, it was loaded. Nodding politely, which was more than Trevelyan did, he walked away.

The encampment seemed eerily untouched by the murder Rep had discovered around eight hours before. Rep didn't know if cops were still circulating among the re-enactors looking for information, but the scene-of-crime team was gone. The Port-A-Potty where he'd found Quinlan's body was nowhere to be seen, but the others were still in place. More re-enactors had arrived, more tents had gone up, and more evidence of horses—much more, Rep thought—had accumulated.

Trevelyan had seemed open and expansive about the medals but evasive and close-mouthed about General Order Number 11—especially when Rep connected it to Lawrence and hinted at a dubious provenance for it. Had Tommy Quinlan gotten his throat cut over that—over some cheesy little twelve-hundred-dollar swindle? Maybe. People were murdered over less every day in America. But, Rep reflected ruefully as he plodded toward the hill leading to Jackrabbit Press, men were murdered a lot more often over women.

Shoulders slumping a bit, he checked his cell phone for messages. There was one, from Melissa. She told him about finding Peter and the police searching the Damons' home. Then her voice flattened a bit, as if to prepare him for anticlimax.

"Finally," she said, "I'm now at the Jackson County Public Library, waiting to talk to Peter's boss. I'm passing the time trying to run down that medal you described. So far I have about six possibilities from as many countries, none of them ours. Talk to you later."

A puffy-eyed receptionist sitting at a polished chestnut desk was the only difference Rep noticed in the front room at Jackrabbit Press. Word of Quinlan's murder had apparently foreclosed any thoughts of clearing away the props from last night's social. The police must have come, but Rep couldn't see any evidence that they were still there.

"I'm very sorry about Mr. Quinlan," Rep told the receptionist.

She nodded as she reached for a Kleenex. He didn't deliberately look at her cleavage as she leaned forward, but a distinctive necklace tucked under her top drew his eye. After a moment's surprise, he realized that the elegant but rather large object dangling from the chain was a DeLorean hood ornament. He averted his glance, both to be polite and to see whether she was wearing a wedding ring. She was.

"Mr. Lawrence says it's like a death in the family," she said, her voice a trifle husky. "In summer, if we weren't gearing up a title, Mr. Lawrence and Tommy and I would often be the only ones here. We're a very small press."

Whose editor-in-chief drove a DeLorean with a knurled walnut dashboard, Rep thought. *And maybe treated the receptionist as a fringe benefit.* He made a mental note of the name on her deskplate: Karin Henderson.

"I'm early for a two thirty appointment with Mr. Lawrence," Rep said then. "I'm Rep Pennyworth."

"He's expecting you in the downstairs conference room," she said.

Rep found Lawrence dressed in a charcoal gray suit with a black tie and a black silk handkerchief. He had a monopoly on mourning garb, for Andy Pignatano, the other man in the room, was wearing a navy blue blazer and a powder blue, open-necked dress shirt. He was within an inch of Rep's modest height and had even less hair, so Rep liked him immediately.

Rep's plan had been to use the conference as a pretext for finding out as much as he could about the investigation thus far. Not a bad idea *per se* but it promptly fell on its face, for Lawrence wasn't going to let a substantive word out of his mouth. Pignatano was there in case Rep wondered how the term "mouthpiece" had come to be slang for "lawyer."

As a result, Rep and Pignatano ended up conversing in a kind of arcane code that lawyers use when they're talking to each other in the presence of clients. For the benefit of readers who aren't lawyers, the following account includes a simultaneous translation into standard English.

"Well," Pignatano said after introductions and distribution of coffee and ice water, "maybe we can start by you bringing me up to date." (*I'll show you mine if you show me yours. You first.*)

"Police searched the Damons' home earlier today and took some things," Rep said. (*We'll start with a tease. Then we'll see.*)

"Including a saber?" (*I want the good parts.*)

"The nosy neighbor who passed this information on didn't specify," Rep said. (*You can't always get what you want.*)

"Well," Pignatano shrugged, "I guess that much was to be expected." (*Come on, you haven't actually told me anything yet.*)

"Really?" Rep said. "Are search warrants that easy to come by in Kansas City?" (*I've told you more than you've told me.*)

"I understand that Mrs. Damon *was* seen talking to the murder victim last night," Pignatano said. (*I can prevaricate as easily as you can.*)

"Sure, but so what? Quinlan was Linda's boss. It'd be natural for them to talk if they ran into each other here. I don't practice criminal law, but it seems a little light in the probable cause department." (*Bullshit.*)

"Maybe," Pignatano said, sketching another shrug. "Or maybe that's not all they had." (*I have to give you something, don't I?*)

"That's my point," Rep said. "Did the cops sell blue sky and sunshine to a judge? Or did they really have something else? And if so, what was it and who gave it to them?" (*Yes, you have to give me something.*)

"Fair questions," Pignatano said, nodding. "In any urban police force you're going to have some cowboys. On the whole, though, the cops here play it pretty straight. I don't think they were just making it up." (*Of course, the cops I know have accounting degrees and go after bank clerks—not guys with Uzis under their tank tops. But you don't know that, do you?*)

"So. What else did they have?" (*Oh yes I do.*)

"Whatever it was," Pignatano said, "they haven't shared it with me." (*I'm not going to out-and-out lie to you, but if I actually tell you the complete truth it will be an accident.*)

"How about you, Mr. Lawrence?" Rep asked. "I know this has been a tough day for you and you have other things to worry about, but have you picked up anything about what's gotten the police interested in the Damons?"

"Andy knows everything I know," Lawrence said.

"Has Mrs. Damon given a statement to the police yet?" Pignatano asked. (*If at first you don't succeed....*)

"Only if she's done it in the last hour or so." (*Figure it out, college boy.*)

"Where is she now?" (*...try, try again.*)

"Are you sure you want to know?" (*Yeah, right.*)

"I don't follow," Pignatano said, smiling in politely feigned puzzlement. (*You don't trust me, do you?*)

"You live here," Rep said. "You have to work with the Kansas City Police Department every day. Neither of the Damons has hired you, at least not yet. Information you get about them right now isn't privileged. I know you wouldn't volunteer it. If a cop happened to ask you, though, that might confront you with a delicate dilemma." (*No, I don't trust you.*)

"True enough," Pignatano said. "One solution would be to have one of them hire me as soon as possible, assuming that's what they want to do." (*Let's fish or cut bait.*)

"You're right, it's not fair to leave you up in the air," Rep said. "Let me check and see if there's any further word." (*Yes, let's.*)

Rep stood up, took out his cell phone, and strolled toward the wall behind Pignatano's chair as he dialed Melissa's number. As simulated ringing sounded in his ears, he pointed the face of the headset at the part of the wall where the mounted medal hung and pushed (or hoped he pushed) a button that would digitally record the image.

"Hello?" Melissa said.

"Nuts, voice-mail," Rep said over his shoulder.

"No, honey," Melissa's voice informed him, "I'm on the phone."

"Melissa, this is Rep. I've been talking with Mr. Lawrence and the lawyer he recommended, Andy Pignatano, who seems very good, and—"

"Reppert, beloved, I am ON THE PHONE. LIVE."

"—I think we need to get Linda in to see him as soon as possible. Have her block out as much of tomorrow as she can."

"Oh, I get it. Sorry to be so slow on the uptake."

"I'll talk to you later."

He ended the call. While he was putting the phone away he squinted at the framed copy of General Order Number 11 on the wall. He just wanted to confirm that General Thomas Ewing's name was at the bottom.

It wasn't. The order was signed by John Rawlins, a general Rep had never heard of.

Have to think about that later, Rep thought as he turned back to the other two.

"Well," he said, "I can't speak for Linda or Peter, of course, but I think you're absolutely right. We need someone who knows what he's doing on their case without delay." (*Which, however, can't be you, because it looks to me like you're somebody else's lawyer.*)

"Thanks for the kind words." (*Even though you were just stroking me.*) "I have a nine o'clock in intake court tomorrow, but I'll have my secretary save as much time from eleven thirty on as I can." (*I'm never going to see these people, am I?*)

After a quick round of moist handshakes and professional smiles, Rep left. On the way out, he took a small notebook and pen from the inside pocket of his sport coat. As he reached the receptionist's desk, though, he decided that a ballpoint pen wouldn't really do for what he had in mind.

"Excuse me," he said to Karin Henderson, "but could I possibly buy a pencil and an envelope from you?"

"No," she said with a smiling-through-the-tears *moue* as she opened the top right-hand drawer of the table. "I will cheerfully *give* you one of each, but only if you promise to take them at no charge."

"We have a deal," Rep said.

He supposed he should have found a handy tree stump to sit on while he composed his message, but decided instead to take the first perch away from Jackrabbit Press that offered itself. This turned out to be the bumper of a school bus parked about halfway down the hill toward the encampment, presumably after delivering a covey of screaming summer-schoolers on a Civil War-theme field trip.

The lined paper in his notebook was anachronistic. He couldn't help that, but he tried to mitigate the problem by turning the notebook sideways and writing across the lines instead of along them. After resisting the urge to lick the pencil point, he set to work:

> My Dear Sgt Pendleton,
>
> I have the honor to request that you make contact with me at your entire convenience to speak further concerning the matter we entered on this morning.

He added his cell phone number, wrote "Esq." with a flourish after his signature, sealed the note in the envelope, and wrote, "Sergeant Red Pendleton, Mo. Partisan Rangers" on the front.

He wandered tentatively toward the Confederate side of the encampment, which was less familiar to him than the Union side. With new participants steadily arriving, what little bearings Rep had lost their meaning in the blossoming of additional tents and swarming of fresh activity. He was wondering whether the copse he was passing through was Yankee or Rebel territory when a gray-clad figure answered the question by stepping out from behind a bush with his musket at port arms.

"Good afternoon, sir!" he bellowed. "Please state your business!"

Startled, Rep jumped back and searched for words. Those that came didn't have a nineteenth-century ring to them, somehow.

"Ah, right. Yes. I, ah, have a message for Sergeant Pendleton of the Missouri Partisan Rangers."

"Sergeant Pendleton is engaged, sir!"

Rep wondered why the picket thought this information would be of interest to people several miles away, where Rep was quite sure the stentorian retort could be heard. Not without some trepidation, he tendered the envelope to the picket.

"Would it be possible, do you think, for someone to deliver this to him when he's free?"

"Corporal of the Guard, post number four!" the picket bawled as he accepted the missive. "Message for Sergeant Pendleton! Corporal of the Guard, post number four!"

"Thank you," Rep said.

"Corporal of the Guard, post number four! Message for Sergeant Pendleton!"

"Much obliged."

"Corporal of the Guard, post number four!"

Rep touched fingertips to his forehead, backed away, and began trudging through the copse toward the parking area where he'd left the Taurus. As he walked, he hoped fervently that the corporal of the guard responded soon.

He told himself that he'd written the note in pencil and used stilted language and old-fashioned diction because he was playing along with the re-enactors, staying in role. It was interesting, though, how readily the words and style had come to him. He thought back to his chat with Melissa about how wearing period clothes and adopting period manners might subtly infuse period attitudes. Peter had been deeply involved in Civil War re-enactment for several years. Could the stern, Old Testament spirit and uncompromising sense of personal honor from that era have infiltrated gentle, self-deprecating Peter, converting him from a dreamy, idealistic logophile into a caricature cuckold, thirsty for vengeance?

Rep was still trying to convince himself he didn't buy it when, about five minutes into his trek, he heard a stampede coming at him through the woods. From the sound of snapping twigs, shredding leaves, and scattering rocks, Rep estimated that a platoon at least was charging in his direction. He hopped behind the biggest tree he could find, hoping that the approaching human tidal wave would roll past him without too much damage.

He managed to hold his curiosity in check for three seconds or so before he peeked around the tree and gazed through the leafy, sunlit maze toward the sound of the thundering rush. Two seconds after that he caught his first glimpse of the racket's source.

It wasn't a platoon.

It wasn't even a squad.

It was Jedidiah Trevelyan. All by himself. Red-faced, pelting, careening, sweeping small animals heedlessly in his wake, pumping his arms, and (in an old Indiana phrase) sweating hard enough to make his own gravy.

"Whoa, hoss," Rep called when Trevelyan had pulled to within ten feet or so. "What's up?"

Trevelyan glared a bit wildly at Rep, then gradually lumbered to a stop. Behind the shelter of Rep's tree, he bent over with his hands on his knees and panted laboriously. Rep gave him a minute or so before he spoke again.

"You okay?" he asked.

"Yeh, just gimme a sec yet," Trevelyan said. "Whoof. I'm gettin' too old to run that fast."

"What were you running from?"

Trevelyan twisted his head enough to look appraisingly at Rep. He squinted, worked his mouth a couple of times as if he were trying to get comfortable with a wad of tobacco, looked back down, then straightened up.

"Summa the boys were doin' a patrol and ambush exercise," he said. "I got in the middle of it without meanin' to and they got a mite cross about it."

"They must be boys who play pretty rough," Rep said.

"True enough, brother," Trevelyan said dismissively.

Rep took out a handkerchief and handed it to Trevelyan, who began mopping his face and neck.

"Much obliged," he said.

"You're welcome."

Rep sat down a few feet away and leaned against a tree. Trevelyan sank to a sitting position himself while he continued to sponge sweat from his face.

"You know," Rep said after another minute or so, "there's a legal concept called fraudulent nondisclosure. You don't necessarily have to lie to cheat someone. Sometimes it's enough if you don't tell the whole truth."

"One more way for lawyers to pick our pockets, I am almighty sure of that," Trevelyan spat.

"We are not a selfless breed, and that's a fact," Rep admitted. "Now, I don't happen to be a great believer in that theory. I think if grown-ups are going to make bargains, they should look out for themselves. Tell the truth, but don't expect me to answer questions you haven't asked."

"Amen to that."

"Juries don't always see it that way, though. I suspect that a lawyer who knows about fraudulent nondisclosure could drum up some business for himself around this encampment if he brought a little energy to it."

Trevelyan was sweating again, and this time not from heat or exertion.

"What's your point?" he demanded.

"I'm not poking my nose into shifty business with Civil War collectibles," Rep said. "I'm not saying you sold Lawrence his copy of General Order Number 11, or that there was something shady about how you came to have that document in the first place, or that Quinlan was in on it, or that any of that has anything to do with him getting his throat cut last night."

"That's what you're *not* saying," Trevelyan said. "Gimme a hint 'bout whatever it is you *are* saying."

"I'm saying that wasn't any patrol and ambush exercise you were running from. I'm saying you were running from the direction of Jackrabbit Press. I want to know why, and if I don't get a straight answer I might start passing out business cards and seeing if the police want to say some of the things I'm not saying."

Trevelyan looked at Rep, and as Rep met the gaze he knew he'd crossed a line. Rep didn't read wariness in Trevelyan's eyes anymore but fear, deep and cold. And his expression suggested not jovial contempt but unadulterated hatred. Rep didn't relax until Trevelyan started to talk.

"First off," Trevelyan said, "you're barking up the wrong tree on that General Order Number 11 business. I don't know where Lawrence bought his copy, but it wasn't from me. Second, you're right about why I was running. I make money off people who don't know the value of things they have. That's just the way it is. Those people are my natural prey. From the way you were talking, I thought this Lawrence fella might be in that category. The first rule is you have to know what you're after before you open your mouth, so I was nosing around the outside of the house and silo and so forth."

"Did Lawrence spot you?"

"Someone did. I heard some boys comin' who sounded like they wasn't happy, so I lit out. I swear to God one of 'em took a shot at me. That wasn't a first in my line of work, and my policy when it happens is to keep goin', so that's what I did. Now that's the God's honest truth, and you can believe it or don't believe it, but I'm goin' back to my store."

Tossing Rep's handkerchief back to him, Trevelyan laboriously rose and waddled off, although he brought a bit more urgency to the task than *waddle* ordinarily connotes.

Rep looked back in the direction the sutler had come from. Fear, common sense, and a gnawing desire to confirm an intuition warred in his psyche. Fear and common sense were on the same side, arguing passionately that the thing to do now was to find a more circuitous route back to the parking area. Gnawing desire won. Shaking his head at his own dubious judgment, he crept cautiously toward the edge of the copse, where Trevelyan had to have entered it.

After he got there it took him a good ten minutes to find what he was after, and even then he almost walked past it without spotting it. Splinters of white wood gouged from under the bark of a sugar maple caught the corner of his eye, and on the double-take he realized he was seeing what he'd been looking for. A bullet—a very real bullet—had ripped into the tree. And from the freshness of the exposed splinter, it hadn't happened too long before. About that much, at least, Trevelyan had been telling the truth.

Rep couldn't remember hearing a shot, but that meant nothing. Between the target range and drill demonstrations to impress tourists, musket and revolver shots had become just one more part of the background noise at the encampment for him. He'd gotten used to them, just as he'd gotten used to scores of men walking around armed to the teeth with real guns.

It took him another twenty minutes to get back to his car. He decided to check the voice-mails on his cell phone before starting the drive back downtown.

"This is Doctor Cerv," the first one said. "I expect to have hard data within the time-frame we discussed. I have a preliminary reading already, however, and I thought I would share it with you orally before putting it in writing." (Rep winced, for coming from expert witnesses these words almost always presaged bad news.) "Findings on the uniform and the dresses you provided are entirely negative. The sword, however, shows substantial human blood residue. The visible blood was wiped away, but enough of it soaked into the metal to leave recoverable elements that put the issue beyond doubt. The blood on the blade is a perfect genetic match with the subject sample on the written report you gave me."

Chapter 16

"Perfect genetic match?" Klimchock said. "This may be more challenging than I thought."

Melissa pursed her lips at this comment, for Rep had cut to the chase the moment she'd answered the phone and she hadn't had a chance to tell her husband that their chat wasn't, strictly speaking, altogether private.

"Melissa, dearest, who was that exactly?"

"That's Diane Klimchock, beloved, Peter's boss at the Jackson County Public Library. I'm in her office, and we're talking on her speaker phone. You may recall you were quite keen when you called on your cell phone a few minutes ago about having a land-line number where you could call me back before we got into the topic of genetics and Dr. Cerv's conclusions."

"Yes, I do remember that. That was because the subject was too sensitive for discussion over a cell phone."

"No worries, luv," Klimchock said briskly. "I'm on your side, and I am discretion its very self."

"Diane pitched in as soon as I explained the situation," Melissa interjected hastily, suspecting that it might be best for Rep to get Klimchock in small doses. "She's helped me slog through all kinds of reference material about medals, and she's come up with some other helpful information as well."

"For example," Klimchock said, "I showed Melissa the minute that Peter left for me when he popped by the library during the small hours."

"Minute being a memorandum," Melissa said.

"I know, dear, I've read all the Smiley novels."

"Peter's note was about the funding campaign for the new library wing," Klimchock said. "We've had a role in mind for Peter, and the gist was that he thought he might not be the right bloke for that billet after all. It's quite a bore because we were planning on sending his capsule bio and prepared testimony in with the dawn patrol today."

"Did he say why he'd gotten cold feet?" Rep asked, wondering whether Peter's note would be Prosecution Exhibit 2 (after the saber) or only Exhibit 27 or so.

"He said he was afraid that he might be an embarrassment to us, but he wanted to talk to me and would try to stop by later in the day."

"It took him forty-eight minutes to write *that*?" Rep asked.

"Well," Klimchock said, "it looks like he may have been rummaging through the files for something but, Peter being such a dear, he left everything neat as a pin, so we can't tell what he was looking for. Also, he left a computer disk with a note saying 'SAVE THIS,' but I beavered away at it for forty-five minutes and it's just half-a-dozen Civil War battlefield maps."

"Diane has left word with the security guard who was on duty to come in half-an-hour early, though," Melissa added, "in case he can fill us in on anything else Peter might have been up to."

"That might help," Rep conceded.

"And speaking of Peter," Melissa said, "he seems to be past the immediate crisis stage, although when I checked in with Linda about an hour ago he was still spending most of his time sleeping and wasn't very coherent when he was awake. The doctor said there were traces of something called flunitrazepam in one of the cups left in the room where we found him."

"I've never heard of that," Rep said.

"The doctor said it was basically valium times ten, according to Linda," Melissa said. "It's sold under the brand name Rohypnol in about sixty countries, although not in this one. At least not legally."

"Hmm," Rep said. "How is Linda holding up?"

"Pretty well, considering," Melissa said. "Now that Peter's out of danger, I think she's happy to have a chance to step up and do something for him. Did you turn up anything more this afternoon, other than Trevelyan being shifty and suspicious and getting shot at?" Melissa asked.

"Andy Pignatano is Lawrence's lawyer," Rep said. "And the receptionist at Jackrabbit Press is named Karin Henderson. With an 'i' instead of an 'e'. I jumped on a couple of very small clues and leaped to the conclusion that she might have had a thing going with the late Mr. Quinlan herself. Maybe she has a jealous husband."

"So we hypothetically have one more alternative suspect?"

"I'll take as many as I can get," Rep said. "General Order Number 11, which is about half the Trevelyan-did-it theory, didn't work out. The document on Lawrence's wall was signed by a General Rawlins instead of General Ewing, so it's not the locally famous one."

"All right," Melissa said, "we'll add Henderson to the list of things we'll be looking into while you're driving back downtown."

"That's my cell phone," Rep said, as a high-pitched ring sounded distantly over the speaker phone in Klimchock's office. "It's probably Sergeant Pendleton, so I'm going to have to ring off and talk to him."

"What are you going to tell him?" Melissa asked.

"That the Kansas City cops picked up my saber instead of Peter's earlier today, and that they can get the one they want at Cerv's lab. Then I'll promise to tell Cerv to turn it over voluntarily, to save the hassle of getting a search warrant in another state."

"Peter, dearest, are you entirely sure that's wise?" Melissa asked.

"That depends on whether Peter is innocent or guilty. If he's guilty—"

"Tommy rot," Klimchock snorted impatiently. "Our Peter is most certainly *not* guilty."

"If he *were* guilty," Rep corrected himself, sighing, "telling Pendleton would be a calculated tactical gamble. If he's innocent, then telling Pendleton is a piece of such elementary good lawyering that not doing it would be close to malpractice. See you soon."

"Right, then," Klimchock said briskly to Melissa as she punched off the speaker phone, "what do we have to occupy ourselves until your skeptical husband shows up?"

"Karin Henderson and Rohypnol, I suppose," Melissa said. "Which I think I can track down. You've been very helpful, but I know you must have tons of work to do in your regular job."

"Peter is a valued employee, and the library expansion has topped my to-do list for two years," Klimchock said. "This *is* my job. Besides, we also have to check out this General Rawlins, who signed an order important enough for Lawrence to have framed a copy of it."

"But Rep said it's the wrong order."

"Nonsense. I'm not throwing away a perfectly good alternative suspect just because the wrong general signed an order. But it does look like long odds, so we'll save that for dessert. To start, I'll do Karin Henderson with an 'i', and you do this glorified sleeping draught."

"Right," Melissa said, partly because it made good sense, and partly because she was quite terrified of saying anything else.

By the time Melissa began mouse-clicks on the Ready Reference computer that Klimchock had made available to her, Rep had told Pendleton about the sabers, and was hearing Pendleton's initial reaction.

"That's very useful information there, counselor," Pendleton said. "I would've said right useful, but Civil War dialect doesn't seem to go with a cell phone, somehow."

"Glad to help," Rep said.

"And I'm real glad I heard this from you before the Metro Squad heard it from Doctor Cerv. Puts a much more pleasant light on things."

"It's like the old story about the farm hand looking for work. The farmer asked him what his qualifications were, and he said he slept well on stormy nights. The farmer understood and hired him."

"Well, I understand too. I'm guessin' that you wouldn't have volunteered this unless that stuff was all clean as a whistle—"

"I have complete confidence in my client," Rep said.

"—although I guess that, even so, I'll mention to one of those Metro Squad boys that if they're not too busy eating doughnuts they might hot-foot it over to Cerv's office first thing tomorrow morning so the crime lab can at least do its preliminary thing sometime before sundown."

"I'll leave a message for Cerv as soon as you hang up, so they shouldn't have any problem."

"Much obliged. As long as you're being so public-spirited and everything, you wouldn't have any idea where Mr. or Mrs. Damon is at the moment, would you? The police can't seem to meet up with either of them."

"That sounds like a question for someone admitted to the practice of law in the State of Missouri," Rep said, "and one of my many limitations is that I personally am not. I understand they're meeting with a lawyer tomorrow, though, and while I don't know how things are done here, I'd expect them to be making formal statements not too long after that."

"A statement that a lawyer has been over is generally about as useful as teats on a boar," Pendleton said, "but you never can tell. Thanks again."

"*Hello*," Melissa said, about a quarter-hour later.

"Something juicy?" Klimchock asked, without looking up.

"Rohypnol is very bad stuff. It causes memory impairment along with low blood pressure, drowsiness and what this entry bashfully calls 'gastrointestinal disturbance.' But it's also called 'the date-rape drug.'"

"I thought gamma hydroxybutyrate was the date-rape drug," Klimchock said. "I looked it up before my last blind date, because a girl can't be too careful these days."

"GHB is also considered a date-rape drug, according to this," Melissa said. "But Rohypnol is becoming more popular because it's legally available in sixty countries, easy to smuggle in, and undetectable if dissolved in a drink."

"Well done, Melissa!" Klimchock said.

"I'm not so sure," Melissa said. "It doesn't speak particularly well of Peter that he had access to that drug, even if he was trying to commit suicide instead of take advantage of an unwilling woman."

"Be your age," Klimchock said dismissively. "Obviously, it was the bimbo who had the drug, not Peter. *She* gave it to *him*."

"Not to lapse into gender stereotypes," Melissa said, "but a bimbo who wants to get a guy into bed generally doesn't have to plan on drugging him."

"The one on TV who tried bedding Peter came a cropper."

"To be sure. But your average, garden variety bimbo wouldn't plan her evening around running into gentlemen like Peter. She'd be anticipating a more readily available male. So why would she go to the risk and expense of getting the one drug she'd never anticipate using? My heart keeps trying to find a way around attempted suicide, but my brain keeps saying no."

"It's my brain that has trouble with the attempted suicide notion," Klimchock said. "I will grant you that suicide is a moral failing, but it does require a certain modicum of physical courage. Now, Peter is a polished jewel, but God love him he is not a courageous man. I've seen him back away from men two stone lighter than he is. I've seen him cringe over paper cuts."

"Something to file away for future reference, I suppose," said Melissa. "Have you turned up anything on Karin Henderson?"

"There is a Henderson who spells her first name that way and lives near Liberty, which would be within easy driving distance of Jackrabbit Press," Klimchock said.

"Is her husband by any wild chance a recently escaped felon who had been serving time for assault-with-intent on an imagined rival?"

"No. He's a shipping expediter with Yellow Freight, and an Air Force reservist on top of it. Not only that, his summer duty includes this week. On Monday night he and his mates got on board a C-140 carrying heavy equipment to Germany, and they're not scheduled to return until Friday."

"So we're down one suspect," Melissa said.

"Never say die, now," Klimchock said. "I'll keep checking, and you track down our General Rawlins and his order."

Melissa had gotten far enough through this latest assignment to learn that General John Rawlins had been chief-of-staff to Ulysses Grant when Rep finally made his appearance. The bravest smile she could muster at her husband's entrance couldn't mask her discouragement.

"Your clever wife has discovered that the toxin which disabled Peter is known as a date-rape drug," Klimchock said, without taking her eyes from her computer screen. "I call that a fair afternoon's work all by itself."

"I'm not so sure," Melissa sighed.

"Maybe we should defer our review of everybody's research for a couple of hours," Rep said. "I think the next order of business is to check in with Linda and Peter. We need to get them into Norm Archer's law office tomorrow morning—and we need to tell them about the saber."

"*Uh* oh," Klimchock said then, still without so much as a glance at Rep, "what have we here?"

"I give up," Rep said.

"Henderson is Karin's married name," Klimchock said.

"Not a member of the Lucy Stone League," Rep said, alluding to the nineteenth-century American feminist who had first called for married women to keep their own names.

"Rep, darling, do quit showing off," Melissa said.

"Her maiden name was Pendleton," Klimchock said. "She's the youngest sister of Sergeant Frederick Pendleton of the Missouri Highway Patrol."

"This somewhat ratchets up the urgency of our talk with Linda and Peter," Rep said.

"It's unanimous," Melissa said.

"We can use my car," Klimchock said.

It was pushing five thirty when the three of them finally made their way into Peter's room at St. Luke's, sixty-plus blocks of rush-hour traffic from the Jackson County Public Library. While Melissa and Klimchock took care of hugging Linda, Rep noted that Peter seemed to be sleeping peacefully, forehead dry and IVs detached.

"The crisis is over," Linda said, following Rep's eyes. "About two hours ago he was able to urinate, and it was like that scene in *Austin Powers* when he wakes up from suspended animation. The doctors were enormously pleased. They told me it meant that the effects of the drug had pretty much worn off. They're going to observe him overnight, and then probably release him in the morning."

"Good," Rep said. "I hate to sound all-business about this, but I think we should go straight from the hospital to Norm Archer's office tomorrow."

"Why?" Linda asked.

As gently as she could, Melissa told her about the residue found on Peter's saber, and the perfect genetic match with Quinlan's blood.

"But that's impossible," Linda said. "It just can't be."

Good defense, Rep thought. *Worked for O.J.*

Rep's phone rang. He stepped out of the room and, seeing signs warning sternly against the use of cell phones in the vicinity of patients' rooms, almost jogged to an open lounge area at the end of the corridor.

"This is Cerv," the voice said when Rep answered. "I wanted you to know that two Missouri Highway Patrolmen left here three minutes ago with the material you brought to me, and the original records documenting chain of custody of said materials from the time it came into my hands."

"Missouri Highway Patrol," Rep repeated. "Not Kansas City, Missouri Police Department or Jackson County Sheriff."

"Correct."

"Is your written report finished yet?"

"It isn't started yet, except for the computer printouts with the raw data, but even if it had been they wouldn't have gotten it. That's work product."

"Right," Rep said. "I'll talk to you later."

Hands clasped behind his back, staring with grim distraction at a mural of Tweety Bird grinning against a garish, red and orange background, Rep stayed in the lounge instead of hurrying back to the room. He told himself that, no matter what, it had been the right decision to tell Pendleton about the saber. The police would have had it within a few days in any event, and this way Peter could be depicted as having nothing to hide. A cynical defense lawyer, seizing on the Karin Henderson née Pendleton angle, might even try to make something out of Sergeant Pendleton sending Highway Patrol troopers instead of local police officers to pick the evidence up.

Right, a minority report in his psyche was saying. *You know what, buddy? You screwed up.* His gut felt hollow.

The police would have a preliminary report on the saber by tomorrow morning at the latest, and maybe within a couple of hours. They might waste an hour checking the Damons' home again, but it wouldn't take them long to start checking hospitals. The next move Rep and company made had to be the right one, and they had to make it fast.

"Who was on the phone?" Melissa asked from behind him a few minutes into his reverie.

"Cerv," Rep said, turning to face her. "Pendleton didn't waste any time. He's already had a couple of his own boys pick up the saber."

"What do you think we should do?"

"I'm not sure, but whatever it is, Linda gets a vote. So let's get her and Dame Diane Klimchock out here to talk things over."

The conference lasted about twelve minutes, which was enough time to come up with three options: (1) wake Peter up and try for an early check-out; (2) stay with Peter until either he woke up and they could talk to him or the police came; and (3) split up, with Rep staying by Peter's bed and the others going back to the library to interview the security guard when he came in early.

For Melissa and Linda, who had seen Peter writhing in his own vomit less than six hours ago, (1) was out of the question. That left (2) and (3). They picked (3), on the theory that if Linda weren't there when and if the police came she, at least, couldn't be interviewed.

They marched back to the room. Peter was gone.

Chapter 17

Klimchock accomplished more in the next three hours than Rep and Linda did—which, unfortunately, wasn't saying much. She drove to her apartment, fed Bloody Helpless (her dog) and Bone Idle (her cat), took Bloody Helpless for a walk, sorted her mail, checked her answering machine, changed from a Modern Career Wear linen skirt-suit and silk blouse into a Casual Moderns linen skirt and cotton blouse, dined on a microwaved pot pie while scanning the *Kansas City Star*, enjoyed a Dunhill and a cup of Earl Grey, and drove back to the Jackson County Public Library. From this she gained a measure of contentment, reinforced adoration from Bloody Helpless, complacent indifference from Bone Idle, and two answering machine questions from John Paul Lawrence, who was wondering whether funding for the Liberty Memorial library expansion project had run into some kind of snag.

Rep and Linda, by contrast, spent their time in the VW checking the Damons' home, Linda's hotel room, the Country Club Plaza, the Kansas City Jazz Museum, Stroud's, Bryant's, the libraries at the University of Missouri-Kansas City and Rockhurst University, and every other haunt and hangout Linda could think of where Peter might have gone to ground. They accomplished absolutely nothing. When Klimchock and Melissa finally reunited with them at the public library guard station shortly before nine thirty that night, they would see a bedraggled, ill-tempered, and empty-handed pair.

For most of this interval, Melissa thought she was faring just about as badly. Linda told her that Chelsea Tuttle stayed at the Raphael Hotel near the Plaza when she visited Kansas City, but a few calls confirmed that she wasn't registered there or in any of the major downtown hotels.

So, *faute de mieux*, Melissa drove the Taurus to the encampment in search of Sergeant Pendleton. Not without difficulty she eventually found the Missouri Partisan Rangers sector of the encampment. She reached that area just after retreat, with plenty of daylight left but no military chores remaining for the re-enactors. So it aggravated her a bit that Pendleton took his own sweet time before moseying over to see her.

"Good evening, Sergeant," she said, choking back her pique and offering a reasonably warm smile. "Thanks for taking the time to talk with me."

"My pleasure, entirely, ma'am," he assured her. Shifting a cast-iron skillet with something sizzling in it to his left hand, he doffed his hat and sketched a hasty bow. "I'm afraid we can't provide any camp stools here."

"Entirely unnecessary," Melissa assured him. With only a hint of clumsiness she sank to a sitting position on the ground, pulling her khaki cotton skirt—definitely not period-authentic—up to her knees. Pendleton tamped down grass with his right foot, then squatted and set the skillet in the flattened space. An inch-thick slab of spit-roasted beefsteak graced the skillet.

"Didn't know if you'd had time to eat," he said, offering her a one-bladed pocket-knife. "We're a bit short on utensils, too."

"That's very kind of you," she said, accepting the knife.

She hadn't quite believed Rep when he'd told her how true believers ate at the encampment. Sensing Pendleton's scrutiny, though, she had no intention of playing greenhorn. Gripping the knife's handle with the lower three fingers of her right hand and bracing her thumb against the dull side of the blade, she sank the edge into the meat, sliced as far as she could, then sawed through a bite-sized piece until she hit iron. She trapped the morsel between her thumb and the blade, raised it to her mouth and dropped it in.

"Delectable," she said after she'd swallowed. "Thanks very much."

"You're most welcome," Pendleton said, nodding slightly. "Now, how may I be of service to you?"

"Well, I don't know if this will be useful to the police, but I thought of something today while we were all trying to recover from the uproar over Mr. Quinlan's death, so I figured I'd pass it along."

"I'd be most grateful if you would."

Melissa let Pendleton watch her enjoy another slice of beefsteak before continuing. The stuff really did taste good, worth even the juice that she could now feel running slowly down her jaw and the grease congealing on her fingers.

"I happened to visit the editorial offices at Jackrabbit Press last night, and saw something a little odd."

"What time were you up there?" Pendleton interjected. No nineteenth-century linguistic flourishes now. All of a sudden it wasn't 1864 anymore.

"I didn't have a watch, but it had to be sometime before ten o'clock. I saw a letter on Mr. Quinlan's chair with a letter-opener stuck through it. Very dramatically, you know, not like the way you'd ordinarily leave a message for someone?" Her voice rose at the end to turn the declaration into a question.

Pendleton's expression didn't change by an eye-blink as she said this. She couldn't tell whether he was holding a pair of deuces or a full house.

"How did you happen to be there?"

"I was with Linda Damon. She works there, of course."

"Right," Pendleton said. "Speaking of Linda Damon, you wouldn't happen to know where she is right now, would you?"

"I couldn't say. Rep told me she's meeting with a lawyer tomorrow, though, so I expect she'll be in touch soon."

"That would be good. Any idea who left this note?"

"It's interesting that you use the word *note*. I saw a letter typed on Jackrabbit Press stationery that I assume Mr. Quinlan signed, but there *was* a note hand-printed over the typing. I didn't recognize the printing, so I'd hate to speculate further. I'd be happy to take another look at it if you'd like."

"Much obliged," Pendleton said. "I'll pass that on to the locals."

"Great. Rep said you were going to have them go over tomorrow and pick up the things he left at Dr. Cerv's lab. I suppose I could meet them there and save time for everyone."

Pendleton's left eyebrow might have twitched a sixteenth of an inch. He offered no other visible reaction.

"I'll mention that possibility to them," he said.

They exchanged farewells and Melissa headed back to her car. After slipping behind the wheel she gave it a frustrated bang with the heel of her right hand. She'd learned something—she just wasn't sure what it was.

Was Pendleton's mention of *note* calculated or inadvertent? Or did he just use it as a synonym for *letter*? Pendleton had asked her nothing about what either the letter or the note said. Did that mean he hadn't known enough about them to appreciate their significance—or did it mean he'd already seen them himself and didn't need her to fill in the blanks? He hadn't told her to sit still while he summoned one of the local detectives working on the case to ask her follow-up questions. Did that mean her information was old news—or did it mean he hadn't told the Kansas City police about sending his own men to Dr. Cerv after lying to Rep about what he was going to do? He hadn't reacted—

"Yipes!"

Surprise as much as fear provoked the mini-yelp. From the corner of her eye she'd caught a shadow passing across her side-view mirror. Adrenaline pumping, she snapped her head around, then sagged back in her seat in anticlimactic deflation. One of the re-enactors on his way back to his own car walked past the Taurus. She was jumping at shadows.

All at once she grabbed the wheel with both hands and pulled herself up straight. The passing re-enactor had white pants, red trim on his collar, and corporal's stripes tips up on his sleeve. Marine, if Rep was right. Probably the only one here, if Rep was right.

As discreetly as she could, she pulled the Taurus out of its parking space, waited until the Marine had gotten his own car under way, and followed him. A thirteen-minute drive brought them both to the Hilltop Motel, where the Marine pulled into a space outside room 125. Melissa parked half-a-dozen spaces away and, by hustling a bit, managed to reach the door just as Chelsea Tuttle opened it to the Marine's knock.

"Good evening, Ms. Tuttle," Melissa said after about five seconds, as no one else seemed interested in saying anything.

"Pennyworth, isn't it?" Tuttle asked in a school-marm voice. "I'm afraid this isn't a very good time. In fact, it's a singularly bad time."

"Would you excuse us for ten minutes, Corporal?" Melissa asked. "I feel awful asking, but it really is terribly important."

The Marine picked up an almost imperceptible nod from Tuttle, touched the bill of his cap, and strode toward a sign that read ICE – VENDING.

"This better be good," Tuttle said. "How did you even know I was here?"

"Finding you was mostly luck. I saw him leaving the encampment, and I remembered that dorm-lounge crack you made last night about your in-depth study of marine biology. I bet on double *entendre* and I won."

"Congratulations." Tuttle stepped away from the door, leaving room for Melissa to come in and close it behind her. "That'll teach me to be clever with editors. I should know better by now."

"Quinlan told you he had a command performance around midnight. Do you know what he was talking about?"

"No. Probably just a standard Tommy fib. The only one at Jackrabbit Press higher on the food chain than I am is John Paul Lawrence himself."

"Did you see Peter or Linda when you left the note in Quinlan's office?"

"Not a sign of either. Anything else?"

"Not much. I don't know if the police have questioned you about that dramatic little note—"

"They've questioned me all right. I walked into it flat-footed. Waltzed over to Jackrabbit Press for my noon meeting and was chatting with a brace of detectives five minutes after I got there. They'd found the letter, they naturally surmised that I'd written the note on it, and they wanted to know all about it. So I told them."

"Did you mention your scene with Quinlan just after you left it?"

"I gave them the PG version. Your name didn't come up, for example, nor that little flick with the riding crop. I thought they might not fully appreciate the ironic turns of a creative mind."

"Perhaps not," Melissa said. "Why did Quinlan's letter infuriate you so much? Most authors would be thrilled to get an offer like that."

"I'm wondering why I should tell you anything more. I give you a hand with that sniveling little weasel and you say thanks by intruding on an intimate evening. Remember, I'm a romance novelist. This isn't just meaningless, empty sex, it's literary research."

"The police haven't questioned me yet," Melissa said. "I haven't had to decide what version of the Quinlan encounter to give them."

"Tell them what you like, honey. Their preliminary guess is that Quinlan was killed between ten thirty p.m. and two thirty a.m. My Marine had to be back by *reveille*, but I have an ironclad alibi from ten at night to at least four thirty in the morning."

"You're not talking to a blushing maiden," Melissa said. "Your ironclad alibi brought a saber with him, and after two bouts of passion he had to be snoring away more than enough time for you to kill Tommy Quinlan and get back to bed."

"You can't really believe I did anything like that."

"I'll decide what I believe after you tell me why his letter got to you."

Tuttle sighed, shrugged, walked over to her bedside table, and poured clear liquid from a crystal decanter into something that looked several cuts above the Hilltop Motel's basic room glass.

"Gin," she said, with a cheers gesture toward Melissa. "Any for you?"

"No, thanks."

"Okay. Jackrabbit Press has no business publishing *Inescapable Courtesy*. Tommy knew it. JP can't get the book reviewed by people who review novels like that and its distribution is all wrong for that kind of story."

"Then why did you offer it to JP?" Melissa asked.

"A formality. JP had a standard option on my next novel. But all it could accomplish by exercising that option on *Inescapable Courtesy* instead of just carrying it over to my seventeenth romance novel was lose a lot of money."

"Apparently Quinlan didn't see it that way."

"He knew exactly what would happen. He picked up the option anyway because he was terrified I was going to blow the franchise. Find a mainstream publisher for *Inescapable Courtesy*, put the book out, and have it bomb."

"Why would that be any skin off his nose?"

"My goodness," Tuttle said. "You may not be a blushing maiden, but you're a *naïf* to the fourth power about the real world of fiction publishing."

"Educate me."

"If *Inescapable Courtesy* crashes and burns, then the beady-eyed little drones at Borders and Barnes and Noble will have permanently embedded in their hard drives that they only sold six hundred thirty-two copies of Chelsea Tuttle's last novel. So when my seventeenth romance comes out, they won't buy any. They won't look to see that the last novel was an ambitious, critically acclaimed, hard-cover experiment in surrealist meta-fiction. All they'll know is that Chelsea Tuttle doesn't sell any more. Those two retailers are a huge chunk of the book business, so JP's cash cow would have dried up."

"Along with your career."

"A risk I was willing to take for the chance to put my name on a piece of serious literature. Escape from the genre ghetto. Win respect as a writer, instead of just a storyteller. Quinlan wasn't."

"But how would having the novel published by Jackrabbit Press instead of a mainstream house solve that problem?" Melissa asked.

"Tommy was going to force me to use a pseudonym. That stuff in his letter about 'just the right marketing approach' was code for that. *Inescapable Courtesy* by an unknown would go nowhere, Jackrabbit Press would take its little bath, and I'd go back to writing about the sentimental education of art history majors. As far as the retailers were concerned, Chelsea Tuttle would still be money in the bank at the paperback rack."

Melissa paused for a moment. Her dogmatic theology was a bit haphazard so she couldn't be sure, but she thought she might be about to commit a mortal sin. She braced herself accordingly.

"If you don't mind," she said, "I'll take you up on that gin after all."

Tuttle shrugged and decanted gin into a second glass—one much more like motel standard issue. Melissa stayed within arm's length of Tuttle after accepting the drink, for the last datum she sought required proximity.

"I can understand why you're so passionate about *Inescapable Courtesy*," she said. "Linda showed me a copy of the manuscript in the office last night, and I read a couple of chapters."

"I'm devastated that you were able to put it down, but at least you got past the first page."

"The concept is very strong. I was just wondering if you were planning on dedicating it to Barbara Kingsolver. That way you might be able to pass it off as an *homage* instead of simple copy work."

A half-glass of gin instantly splashed Melissa's face. Even with stinging eyes and sopping eyelids, Melissa saw Tuttle's slap coming in ample time to avoid it. Instead of ducking, though, she let Tuttle's open hand smack her right cheek, felt the skin burn as a fiery blush rose to her ear.

"Not bad," Melissa said appraisingly. "But it didn't rattle my teeth the way mom's used to. You're going to have to put more wrist into it if you want to impress someone who grew up in the lower Midwest. All the same, I'm glad you didn't have a knife handy."

"You can tell me my story stinks out loud if you want to," Tuttle said, gasping with rage, "but every word in it is mine and mine alone. It means everything in the world to me. Now get out!"

"I'll take your word for it," Melissa said. "I was lying when I said I'd read part of it. I'm sorry for that, and for accusing you of plagiarism. I was trying to provoke you because I wanted to know how violent you could get on sheer impulse. Now I do."

"Don't be an ass," Tuttle said, her tone dismissive but her voice shaky.

"It wouldn't have made sense for you to leave a lurid note for Quinlan and then assault him in front of a witness if you were *planning* on killing him. But say he ended up reaching you on your cell phone and talking you into a little improvisational chat in the small hours after all. If he said something that pushed the wrong button when you had a blade within reach, you might have lashed out at him without thinking about it at all."

"I see. And how did I get his body to the privies?"

"With some help from your alibi, maybe. Or maybe you went to the privies for the chat in the first place."

Tuttle turned three-quarters away from Melissa, shrugging her shoulders in a combination of resignation and contempt.

"I don't apologize for the slap," she said in a bored voice. "You had it coming. I do regret sloshing you, because that was a waste of perfectly good gin. Now clear out."

Melissa cleared out. Her cheek still smarted as she swung the Taurus through a gravel-spitting turn out of the hotel parking lot. Instead of rubbing the sting away she clung to the pain, for it cemented her conviction that Chelsea Tuttle could have killed Quinlan. The theory had some loose ends, but so did every other theory except Peter-did-it. Tuttle's alibi was worthless. And don't tell me a woman wouldn't kill that way, she warned an imaginary challenger. Remember Marat during the French Revolution? He didn't die in his bath from old age, did he?

That's when a chill that had been creeping unnoticed through her gut began to surface. Not, at first, an appalled shock. More like the slowly dawning anxiety you feel when you begin to wonder whether you left your wallet at the restaurant two exits back.

No, she told herself scoffingly. *It couldn't—*

But instead of going away the dread inside her grew until it exploded like a rupturing appendix.

NO! she screamed mentally, squeezing the wheel in a white-knuckled spasm. Shrugging off the shrill denial, though, her brain kept pitilessly spitting out questions that pained her far more than Chelsea Tuttle's slap.

Speaking of alibis, where was Linda between, say, one and three a.m.?

NO!

She said she was looking for Peter, but aside from Nichols on Broadway how many all-night places could there be in Kansas City?

NO! her heart raged.

That would be the Linda who'd said, "If it turns out I'm carrying the baby of that scum-under-a-rock editor I'm going to be ready to kill someone."

NO! Linda is kind, gentle, smart, and idealistic!

Right, her brain muttered coldly. *And so was Charlotte Corday.*

Chapter 18

Security officer Lafayette Wyatt appeared, as promised, half-an-hour before his shift. Rep guessed his age at twenty-five or so. Short-cropped black hair bristling above his dark brown skin seemed to emphasize his youth. His shoes weren't just shined but polished to a high gloss, and his equipment belt gleamed. From a gold chain around his neck dangled a plain gold cross and a red numeral one—whether in tribute to Jesus or the First Infantry Division Rep wasn't sure.

"I'd noticed the lady hanging around outside for a good half-hour before Mr. Damon came back down," he said after Klimchock had gotten him into the topic. "And that's not your everyday thing, o' course, a lady like that by herself after midnight on the sidewalk in downtown Kansas City. I mean, at first I was thinkin'—well, you know what I was thinkin'—but a coupla guys passed her by, and she didn't make a move."

"What did she look like?" Rep asked.

"Well," Wyatt said earnestly, "she looked like a girl from a shampoo commercial, is what she looked like. She had this blond hair, not like hair you usually see on women just walking around, sorta live and swingy, and the one time she smiled she had, like, this flash that really grabbed you. And she seemed kind of underweight, but with real big, you know, and like these long, tan legs, and fu— uh, that is, real sassy kinda shoes."

"So then Mr. Damon came down," Klimchock prompted.

"Right. And he signed out and we said good night, and I could tell he noticed the lady. Kinda glanced over at her and did a double-take, you know? Then he walked on out. Now it was hot and sticky, so I had the outside sliding window on the guard cubicle about halfway open and I could hear what she said to him as soon as he hit the sidewalk. She didn't waste any time at all."

"And what did she say to him?" Klimchock asked, giving precisely equal emphasis to each syllable.

"Oh, she was all, 'I'm visiting from outta town and I met some friends for dinner and drinks and then we all started to take a walk and they peeled off one by one and all of a sudden I was by myself and I realized I'd gotten lost like the ditz I am'—she shook her hair when she said that part, an' I'll tell you, one look at that girl an' I could tell she'd never walked more'n three blocks before at one time in her life. Anyway, could Mr. Damon get her back to her hotel? And he says yes, and they walked off to where he'd parked his car on the street."

Melissa and Linda exchanged glances. There was only one male over fourteen that either of them knew who could possibly have fallen for that story.

"Thank you very much, Laf," Klimchock said.

"Glad to help out."

"Well," Linda said to Melissa, Rep, and Klimchock as Wyatt headed for the break room, "it must have been an excruciatingly long day for you three, and I don't think we can accomplish anything else until tomorrow morning. Should we call it a night, get me back home in case Peter calls or comes by?"

"I most certainly do *not* think we should call it a night," Klimchock said. "There is work to be done yet, leads to track down, loose ends to tie up. I should say we have miles to go before we sleep."

Melissa had to hide a scowl, for what she'd wanted most since she'd hit the freeway ninety minutes ago was time alone with Linda.

"Well," she said dubiously as the quartet began moving toward the elevator, "we have the medals to finish up, and General Rawlins, but they shouldn't take long."

"Don't forget Anita Lay, or whoever she really is," Linda said.

"Anita Lay?" Rep asked.

"That was the name on the registration card at the Palm Gardens Hometel," Melissa explained with the hint of a sigh. "I can't fit her in with Jedidiah Trevelyan or Red Pendleton or anything else we've learned, but after the story we just heard I guess we can't ignore her."

"If it's a phony name, though," Klimchock said, "how can we find anything out about her tonight? Whom do we know who could fill us in on what I'm guessing is a very shady call girl from out of town?"

Without turning her head, Melissa shifted her eyes toward Rep. He met the stealthy gaze. They were thinking the same thing: *Mom.*

"Actually," Rep said, clearing his throat in an unsuccessful attempt to sound casual, "if you can show me to a land-line telephone where I can make and receive long-distance calls, I might be able to take a stab at it."

"Aces!" Klimchock said. "You can use the phone in the acquisition head's office. Computer too. She's over budget anyway, so it won't matter."

Microfilm readers, vertical files, and heavily laden shelves crowded the third floor, but Klimchock navigated its dark expanse with serene confidence. She led Melissa and Rep into a small office, knew the password necessary to boot up the computer, and punched a complex billing code into the phone.

"There you are," she said to Rep as a dial tone sounded over the receiver she handed to him. "Nine-one-area code and off you go." Then, taking Linda literally in hand, Klimchock headed toward her own office.

Rep had long since stopped blushing at the recorded message on his mother's answering machine—*if you've been naughty... if you require an attitude adjustment…leave a number….*—but he still waited with visible impatience for the phrases to end and the beep to sound.

"This is Spoiled Sibling," he said, using a pseudonym she'd suggested, in case she didn't recognize his voice. "I'm interested in someone who might use the name Anita Lay, blond, mid-twenties, *California Girl* look, recently out of town. You can call me back at this number for the next ninety minutes."

"Well," Melissa said as she mouse-clicked two feet away, "that's done."

"What are you working on?" he asked.

"General Rawlins," she said. "While it's printing I'll pop Peter's disk in and you can look over my shoulder and see if you can make anything out of the battlefield maps."

Rep gazed dutifully at the screen while Melissa clicked through the images. He frowned in concentration and bafflement.

"Spotsylvania…Cold Harbor…Petersburg…Jubal Early's Valley campaign…Fisher's Hill…Cedar Creek," Rep murmured thoughtfully. "Kind of a mixed bag. Well-known battles that were bloody but indecisive, and then a couple I can barely remember at all."

"Do you see any kind of pattern?"

"They were all fought in 1864, fairly close to Washington. Maybe I'll be able to make something out of this after I sleep on it. What did you find about General Rawlins?"

"Hi," said Linda, who picked that moment to appear in the doorway with a handful of paper. "Diane told me to bring these down to you. They're printouts of the medals that looked like they might match Rep's description. Now Rep can look at them and see if one of them does."

"Didn't you get the picture of the medal that I sent to you?" Rep asked Melissa as he accepted the sheets.

"What I got, actually," Melissa said, "was a picture of what looked like a junior accountant at Enron being taken on a perp walk. I couldn't help wondering why you'd passed it on."

"Nuts," Rep said. "And I was so proud of myself. I was thinking of ordering my next martini shaken and not stirred. He's not a junior accountant at Enron, by the way, but he was being taken on a perp walk."

"Who was he?" Melissa asked.

"A member of the French Resistance executed by the Nazis," Rep said. "What did Lawrence say his name was? Give me a second. Brassilach, that's it. Robert Brassilach."

"What?" Melissa yelped.

"Robert Brassilach," Rep repeated. "Lawrence said he was an outstanding poet, novelist, and critic."

"He was right," Melissa said.

"And that he was shot by a firing squad in France during World War II."

"Also true," Melissa said.

"He said he was shot essentially for editing a newspaper."

"Right again," Melissa said. "Except he wasn't shot by the Nazis. He was executed by the French. The newspaper he edited was a collaborationist sheet called *Je Suis Partout*—I Am Everywhere. One of the more charming things he wrote was, 'We have to separate ourselves from the Jews as a whole, and not keep the little ones.' At his trial he said he just wanted mothers and children to stay together."

"The French shot him for that?" Rep asked. "Didn't think they had it in them. But how do you happen to know about it?"

"Among literary academics the Brassilach case is a famous study in the conflict between freedom of expression and the moral responsibility of intellectuals for what they write. Alice Kaplan described his trial in a book called *The Collaborator*. You can get a pretty good argument at your average academic conference that, no matter how reprehensible his words were, Brassilach shouldn't have been executed for publishing them, even in wartime."

"'Should I shoot the poor boy who deserts the colors, and leave unmolested the editor whose words caused him to run away?'" Rep said.

"Who said that, DeGaulle?"

"Abraham Lincoln, concerning the arrest of a copperhead newspaper editor during the Civil War."

"You're showing off again," Melissa said.

"It must be contagious."

"Linda," Melissa said, "forget about those medal pictures you have. Dig the book out again and see if it has any entries for Vichy."

"What are we saying?" Linda asked. "That Lawrence is a crypto-Nazi?"

"I think that might be a bit of a leap from one odd picture," Rep said.

"I don't know about crypto-Nazi, but we have more than a picture to suggest pathological anti-Semite," Melissa said as she grabbed a page from her computer's printer. "Look at this. Missouri isn't the only place that had a famous General Order Number 11. General Grant also issued one that was signed by his chief of staff, General John Rawlins."

Linda and Rep pressed around Melissa to read the page she held:

> The Jews, as a class violating every regulation of trade established by the Treasury Department and also department orders, are hereby expelled from the [D]epartment [of the Tennessee] within twenty-four hours from the receipt of this order. Post commanders will see to it that all of this class of people be furnished passes and required to leave, and any one returning after such notification will be arrested and held in confinement until an opportunity occurs of sending them out as prisoners, unless furnished with permit from headquarters. No passes will be given these people to visit headquarters for the purpose of making personal application of trade permits.

"According to the note on this website," Melissa said, "the Department of the Tennessee included Tennessee, Kentucky, and Mississippi. So Grant's General Order Number 11 exiled all the Jews in three states under military occupation. Lincoln made Grant rescind the order a few weeks later."

"Maybe we're going too fast," Linda said. "Mr. Lawrence is cultured, sophisticated, literate, generous, and well-mannered."

"So was Brassilach," Melissa said. "And he sat serenely in his office and called for Jewish children to be rounded up and sent to death camps."

"Well," Rep said, "I'm duly taken aback. I think we've peaked. Tonight isn't likely to generate any further information quite as dramatic as this."

The phone rang.

Rep answered it with a simple "Hello." No name or place. That was the way fate had decreed he would talk on the phone to his own mother. The caller dispensed with preliminaries as well.

"I've seen the name Anita Lay in the credits for so-called quality adult films, but I suspect it's generic, not the screen name of a particular actress."

"'Quality' adult film as opposed to what kind?" Rep couldn't help asking.

"As opposed to quickies for specialty tastes, like my clients have, which are basically infomercials, and garden variety skin-flicks that just get right down to it. Quality are longer running, with actual story lines, dialogue—even multiple camera angles. Some actors and actresses get famous starring in movies like that. They have regular screen names, and they use them in movie after movie. Others, though, are just paying the rent while they wait for Quentin Tarantino to cast them in something legitimate. They show up in the credits under generic names that are usually lame puns—like Anita Lay. The actresses change, but the names stay the same."

"What's 'Anita Lay' a pun for?" Rep asked. "*Oh*. Never mind."

"Right."

"So, in other words, the particular woman we're wondering about could be any blonde in her early twenties."

"Well, not just any blonde. She's almost certainly an aspiring actress living in southern California."

"Why do you say that?" Rep asked. "Why couldn't she just have picked the name up from watching some, er, quality adult films?"

"Oh come on. These aren't exactly chick-flicks, are they? And even the guys who watch them couldn't tell you any name in the credits after the second line. GET YOUR NOSE BACK IN THAT CORNER THIS SECOND, YOUNG MAN! YOU'RE BEING PUNISHED AND YOU'RE IN DISGRACE! Sorry, that last part wasn't directed at you. I have a client here."

"Understood," Rep said. "I see your point. Still, 'aspiring actress living in southern California' doesn't narrow it down very much."

"I'll tell you one thing," the caller said. "Any wannabe starlet who leaves LA for KC in June is looking for a fat payday."

"Where would the payday come from?"

"A sugar daddy who'd have a limo meet her at the airport, put her up in the best suite in the best hotel in town, and plan on spending a weekend's worth of quality time with her."

"Doesn't fit," Rep said. "Unless there are sugar daddies with a taste for date-rape drugs."

"What did you just say? This chick was feeding ropes to johns?"

"If 'ropes' means Rohypnol, that super German sleeping pill that guys sometimes slip into cocktails, then that's what she was doing."

"That's what 'ropes' means. Well, that makes it obvious, doesn't it?"

"To half of us, apparently," Rep said.

"She wanted to get a guy into what we used to blushingly call a compromising position. Find someone in Kansas City who could be blackmailed into tucking a billion-dollar tax-break into a budget bill or quashing a drug investigation, and I'll bet you've found Anita Lay's target."

"How about someone who could sell ten million copies of *Star* magazine by being shown on the cover with his pants down?" Rep asked.

"Bingo."

"Thanks." Rep hung up and summarized his mother's well-informed conclusions for Linda and Melissa.

"You mean whoever she was, she came here just to set up a phony picture of Peter committing adultery?" Linda asked.

"Sure," Rep said. "Peter became an instant mini-celebrity for turning down a proposition on television. You can bet some scandal sheet would pay middle five figures for pictures that it could headline '*REALITY CHECK'S* "GOOD" HUSBAND CAUGHT IN LOVE NEST.'"

"That's why Peter thought he'd done something terrible," Linda sniffled, near tears again but this time from happiness. "Not because he'd killed Quinlan. Because of the drug he couldn't remember exactly what happened, but he remembered enough to think he'd been unfaithful to me."

"I'd bet that way," Melissa said. "But she presumably got her pictures, so you two are going to have to brace for a couple of weeks' worth of ugly ink."

"Well," Rep said modestly, "the intellectual property bar might have something to say about that."

"You mean threaten to sue them for libel?" Melissa asked skeptically.

"No, I mean threaten to libel them."

"You're being opaque again, dear."

"I have the e-mail address of the general counsel for every tabloid in the country," Rep said.

"Do they all owe you favors?" Linda asked.

"They'll think they do after I pass on a hot tip that police in Kansas City are looking into charges of second degree sexual assault involving the drug-assisted rape of Peter Damon by a self-proclaimed starlet who let slip that she was working for their papers."

"But only one of them is guilty," Melissa said.

"That's what makes it libel. The ones that aren't guilty will start chasing down the story. The paper that actually gave that bimbo an advance will know that its rivals will crucify it if it runs the story. Which it wouldn't anyway, once its lawyers told it about accessory before the fact, aiding and abetting, criminal conspiracy, and extradition. It might not work, but it's sure worth a shot."

Melissa saw Linda's face come alive with a gently radiant glow. *She loves deeply and fiercely,* Melissa thought. *She could have killed for that love.* But Melissa banished all thought of cross-examining Linda or checking the VW's odometer. Sometime in the last twenty minutes, she'd made a decision. *I love justice,* Camus had said, *but I'd defend my mother in court.* Guilty or innocent, Linda was her friend. Guilty or innocent, she needed Melissa's unqualified and unconditional support, and guilty or innocent she'd have it. If Linda had killed Quinlan, someone else was going to have to prove it.

For the first time since she'd realized Tuttle was going to slap her, Melissa's shoulders relaxed. They stayed relaxed for almost five seconds. Until the scream.

Chapter 19

"Stop him! Don't let him get to the west stairwell!"

This command came out of the darkness in Klimchock's piercing contralto as Rep, Melissa, and Linda rushed into a halo of light outside the acquisition head's office. Rep had no idea where west was. He vaguely recalled that row upon row of seven-foot metal shelves holding books and bound periodicals started perhaps fifteen feet away. Beyond that, he didn't have the first clue about the layout of the mostly pitch black third floor of the Jackson County Public Library.

He groped his way toward the first row of shelving and then down that row, away from the sound of Klimchock's voice, to a wide aisle running along the ends of the rows. He began to jog cautiously down this aisle and had passed the ends of three rows when, incredibly, he heard the *thump-thump* of running feet hustling along a parallel aisle on the other end of the rows.

Two, three, four more rows and then abruptly he lost the sound. He backtracked a row and picked the *thumps* up again, a bit fainter this time, as if the runner were now moving away from him. He turned and began running between two rows, toward the aisle at the other end and, presumably, another set of shelves beyond that aisle.

As his eyes adjusted to the blackness he was able to make out a dim suggestion of a figure running only thirty or forty feet ahead of him. Rep didn't regard himself as particularly athletic. He'd once joked about timing a three-mile jog with a calendar, and no one had laughed. Astonishingly, though, he sensed himself gaining on the runner. Within a dozen strides he had crossed the intervening aisle and halved the distance separating him from his quarry. He began to wonder what he might do if he actually caught the guy (or, he supposed, gal).

The runner started pulling books from the shelves to the floor as he ran, presumably in an effort to impede Rep's pursuit. Rep stumbled a couple of times, but at the end of the row the runner slowed to turn down the intersecting aisle and suddenly Rep was less than ten feet from him. Rep reached for everything he could to quicken his pace.

Suddenly the runner whirled in Rep's direction. At that instant, Rep's right instep hit a thick tome and he found himself airborne and horizontal. He saw a muzzle flash and heard the booming *POW!* of a gunshot. Shortly after that he was still horizontal but no longer airborne, for gravity had performed in its predictable way and he sprawled painfully on the linoleum floor.

Rep scrambled to his feet but then immediately fell to one knee as his throbbing right ankle gave way. The lights came on. An alarm bell began to ring. He heard scurrying steps—behind him, this time—and turned to see Klimchock, Melissa, and Linda hurrying toward him through a swarm of black dots. He began to drag himself toward the end of the row, in the faint hope that he could at least glimpse the fugitive now that the lights were on.

"No, no, dear," Klimchock said, laying a restraining hand on his shoulder as she came up and knelt beside him. "Discretion the better part of valor and all that. He has a gun and we don't, so he wins this round. End of issue, full stop. Remember, the spirit of Dunkirk is running away so that you can fight another day. Besides, that alarm means that he's opened the emergency door at the bottom of the west stairwell. He's long gone."

"You're absolutely right," Rep said.

"Are you hurt?" Melissa asked.

"Dinged my ankle," Rep admitted.

"That must have been a nasty fall," she said.

"A lucky one, though," Rep said. He had by now gotten his shoe and sock off and was examining his swelling ankle. "Without my stumble that bullet might have hit something important."

Melissa glanced down the aisle at the thick tome he'd stumbled over. The title on the spine read *Burr*.

"How ironic," she said. "The greatest service Gore Vidal has ever rendered to American literature is saving your life."

"That's a sweet thing to say," Rep said, managing a wan smile.

"You obviously haven't read much of Mr. Vidal's work," she said.

"With the alarm and the shot, police will be here soon," Rep said. "It might be best if Linda were somewhere else when they arrived."

"Just so," Klimchock said. "So perhaps I was here alone."

"Up to a point, Lord Zinc," Melissa said.

"That means 'no,'" Linda explained to Rep. "It's from Evelyn Waugh."

"Right," Rep said to Klimchock. "You were here with all three of us when we talked to Lafayette Wyatt and when we all left time-of-use data on telephones and computers on this floor."

"Then what happened?" Klimchock asked. "In case the bobbies ask."

"Then," Melissa said, "I think Linda had to help me take Rep somewhere to care for his ankle. While you waited for the police."

"Right, got it," Klimchock said, focusing as intensely as if she were prepping for her final in Greats at Oxford. "And where did you go?"

"Uh, *well*," Rep said, "you don't know that, do you?"

"No, of course not. Ah, right, got it. Off you go then, to wherever."

◇◇◇

"It can't be a coincidence. We've been thinking about this whole problem backwards."

Rep muttered this statement rather drowsily about forty-five minutes later. Pillows propped him up in the bed in Linda's hotel room, his right ankle clumsily wrapped in ice-cube stuffed towels and his neurons sedated with Advil.

"What can't be a coincidence and what do you mean backwards?" Melissa asked, not unreasonably.

"I've heard a fair number of live gunshots in my life, from duck hunting to sighting-in to the encampment," Rep said.

"And a shotgun doesn't sound like a rifle or a rifle like a handgun, I'm betting," Melissa said.

"Not only that. A thirty-thirty doesn't sound like a thirty-aught-six, and neither of them sounds like a rifled musket. The gunshot tonight sounded like the revolvers I heard on the firing range at the encampment. No judge would let my impression into evidence, but you can take it to the bank. The intruder's gun was a Civil War era replica revolver."

"Honey," Melissa said, "maybe you'd better get to the backwards part."

"We've been assuming that Quinlan getting killed while Peter was out there for the encampment is some kind of grotesque coincidence. Assume that it's not a coincidence—that, it's all connected."

"I'm assuming," Linda said. "I'm not getting anywhere."

"Sometime after you took Peter upstairs last night, Peter saw something totally unexpected that sent him hurtling away the moment he was certain you were all right. What was it?"

"Well, beloved," Melissa said, "we don't know, do we?"

"Yes we do. It was a problem with the library expansion funding, and Peter's role in getting it. That's what he said in his note to Klimchock."

"Which leaves only the detail that we don't know exactly what the problem was," Linda pointed out.

"That's right," Melissa said, snapping her fingers, "but we do know it must be something very dramatic in the editorial offices and that it's related to what got Quinlan killed, with Peter neatly framed for the murder."

"And we know that—how?" Linda asked.

"Because otherwise it's coincidence," Rep said, "and I'm not buying it."

"So all we have to do," Melissa said brightly, "since the police would laugh in our faces just before they arrested us if we went to them with this, is figure out for ourselves what Peter saw."

"Well," Rep said, "for a group that just accounted for Gore Vidal's single greatest contribution to American literature, that should be a piece of cake."

Chapter 20

"Welcome to the house that crack built," Norm Archer said as he showed Rep, Melissa and Linda into his office—or into what Rep took to be his office, for it might have passed as easily for a small law library or a large storeroom. Two library tables scarred with nicks and cigarette burns formed a T toward the near wall of the high-ceilinged room. Hard-bound volumes of Vernon's Annotated Missouri Statutes and West's Southwest 2d Reporter lined the walls. No water, coffee, or ashtrays. Archer apparently didn't want his typical clients to linger.

He pointed his visitors to chairs on either side of the T's leg and seated himself at its apex. Folding hands two shades darker than a grocery sack in front of him after he'd adjusted his white suspender straps a quarter-inch on each shoulder, he looked at each of them in turn with coolly appraising eyes, neither judgmental nor accepting. Late forties or early fifties, Melissa thought. Bristly white hair, more than a hint of a paunch, but definitely not fat.

"All right," he said in a voice that suggested a drill sergeant slightly (but only slightly) mellowed by age and miles, "what do we have?"

He heard them through twice, the first time without questions and the second time with. He didn't take a note from beginning to end. Below the neck, in fact, he scarcely moved at all.

"You have no idea where Peter is?" he asked after the encore.

"Right," Linda said.

"Well, I expect we'll know soon," Archer said. "In a job-one case like this the cops will have a preliminary report on that saber by ten o'clock—and it sure won't take *them* long to find him. Unless he's flown the coop."

"No," Linda said, shaking her head. "Peter wouldn't run."

"He won't run far, that's for sure," he muttered. Then, abruptly twisting his head over his right shoulder toward the office door, he raised his voice to bark, "Streeter. Miss Phelps."

A white man in his early twenties and a grandmotherly African-American woman answered the summons, which had apparently penetrated the substantial door without difficulty.

"Monitor the police band on short wave," he told the man. "Any chatter about arresting Peter Damon, I wanna know A-sap. All we can do is hope he keeps his mouth shut until I talk to him. Miss Phelps, please take these ladies down to the coffee shop, get them something to drink. Mrs. Damon is giving blood this morning and she should have some fluids beforehand."

Melissa raised her eyebrows at Rep—*What is this, the last scene of* The Godfather? He tried to shrug apologetically with his. After a moment of delicious tension she acquiesced. Once the women had filed out, Archer strolled across the office to a window looking over Thirteenth Street and McGee in downtown Kansas City. He clasped his hands behind his back. Gold lettering on the window read NORM ARCHER ATTORNEY AT LAW. Sunlight streaming through the window projected the R and the C across his chest.

"Trevelyan is the best bet," he said. "His motive sounds like a reach, but Pendleton is a cop and Tuttle's a woman. For some damn reason American juries will *not* believe that a white woman killed someone with a blade."

"Even though Lizzie Borden orphaned herself with an axe and Lana Turner's daughter took out Johnny Stompanato with a knife," Rep commented.

"They both walked," Archer said. "Still, three alternative suspects is better than none. One of them might even be guilty."

"Might?"

"Oh, odds are your boy did it," Archer said.

"I don't think he did, but I can't argue about the odds."

"Cops here are straight-ahead guys," Archer said. "They'll lie through their teeth to keep a low-life from beating a rap on some picky technicality like the United States Constitution, but they wouldn't take a twenty to drop a speeding ticket even if there wasn't any milk in the house. They're gonna go with the odds. This anti-Semitism/library expansion stuff—forget about it. Even if I'd gotten the Damons in here yesterday morning and worked out statements for them without any disappearing acts, Peter would be the prime suspect. As it is, there's no way they're looking at anyone else."

"So. You want the case?"

"You kidding?" Archer swiveled and gave Rep something just south of a grin. "This is a dream case for a guy like me. Respectable client—maybe he killed someone, but the guy had it coming. And at least he doesn't sell smack to school children. Brave wife sitting in the front row in her Sunday best. Enough money to do a full-scale, no-stone-unturned investigation. TV cameras lined up outside the courthouse after trial each day. Couple of twists the right jury might get its teeth into."

"On the other hand," Rep prompted.

"On the other hand, seems to me there's an alternative suspect we haven't talked about yet. Motive, opportunity, no alibi, and explains the blood on the saber very nicely. That's why I wanted to have this chat stag."

"Linda?" Rep demanded in astonishment as he parsed the comment. "That's impossible. Linda couldn't—"

"I know, I know," Archer sighed. "You know her and she couldn't have done it. I hear that in almost every homicide rap I handle. Murder is supposed to be committed by kids from the 'hood and stone cold gangsters like we see in the movies. We can't imagine a normal guy who mows his lawn and whistles while he carries the garbage out or a cheerful matron who clips coupons and fusses over laundry committing murder. But they do, my friend, oh yes they do. Murder is the ultimate amateur crime. You tell me Linda Damon couldn't knock over a gas station or hustle crack, I'll listen. Don't tell me she couldn't kill a guy who endangered her marriage by using her for cheap sex."

"That could be a complicated defense to present," Rep said dryly, thinking of the brave wife in her Sunday best suddenly quailing under the accusatory finger of the lawyer she herself had hired.

"If it were easy Andy Pignatano could handle it. But I don't want it any more complicated than it has to be. So tell me why I'm wrong about Linda. Or about Peter, for that matter. Tell me why it isn't one or the other."

"The blood that isn't there," Rep said. "No blood on the uniform *or* the dress. Whoever killed Quinlan all but decapitated him, drenched the saber in blood. How did either Peter or Linda do that without splattering a drop on their own clothing?"

"Fair point. The state will have an expert talk about blood spatter patterns and angles of dispersion, but thank God juries have common sense. Anything else?"

"Well, it sure wasn't Linda who took a shot at me in the library last night when I got too close."

"The state might say that didn't happen at all, unless the bullet turns up—and there's no guarantee it will. You look like an honest guy, but I'd lie to save a buddy's butt and I'll bet you would too. And the shooter coulda been Peter anyway. He'd certainly know the library well enough to find an obscure exit stairwell in the dark. With the lights off, maybe he didn't know who he was shooting at. And don't kid yourself: I could square that one with either Linda or Peter cutting Quinlan."

"If it's either one of them, though," Rep said, "we have a two-piece puzzle: a tawdry fling and a bloody saber."

"Nice and simple," Archer said. "The way most murders are."

"Nice and simple, though, leaves a lot of pieces unaccounted for. And not just the anti-Semitism pieces."

"Maybe we're actually sneaking up on reasonable doubt," Archer said. "What pieces would those be?"

"The money pieces. Jackrabbit Press publishes maybe eight titles of paperback-original genre fiction every year. Say eight-ninety-five each retail, to be generous. That means Jackrabbit Press sells them for less than five bucks a pop, with a gross profit of maybe two dollars per copy."

"So what? I thought Jackrabbit Press did lots of other stuff besides the bodice-rippers to make money."

"It does," Rep said. "The D and B I looked over when I prepared my pitch to Lawrence said it gets millions a year in overseas printing and distribution work, mostly from Indonesia, Malaysia, and Saudi Arabia."

"So there's your money pieces right there."

"Not really. Unless John Paul Lawrence is publishing paperbacks as a hobby the bodice-rippers still have to pay their own way. How could it make sense for Jackrabbit Press to pay Tommy Quinlan DeLorean wages? How could it think about paying me a hundred thousand dollars just to defend a possible exclusive right to use this fictional military unit to promote Civil War romance novels? They'd have to sell fifty thousand *additional* copies just to break even—and that's before they've spent a penny on the make-believe soldiers themselves. A romance novel that sells fifty thousand copies total is a pretty big deal. Those let's-pretend soldiers would have to turn two or three titles into mega-hits just to pay the legal bill. Put that together with Quinlan having some kind of mysterious midnight meeting and what do you have?"

"I don't know," Archer said. "Drug dealing? Money laundering? Or maybe just a boss who had to get a party over with before he could hold a production scheduling meeting that couldn't wait."

"Like I said. Puzzle pieces."

"When the O.J. verdict came down," Archer said, pursing his lips, "I was driving back to KC from St. Louis. I'd had an argument in the Eighth Circuit Court of Appeals that morning, and the news hit about ten miles onto I-70. All the way back I heard call-in radio feedback on the verdict. The only other time I heard anger like that was after nine-eleven."

"I can imagine," Rep said.

"Thing is, the callers weren't mad because a brother had beaten the rap. They were mad because a *rich guy* was gonna walk. O.J. Simpson stood for every time they'd had the electricity turned off for missing a payment, every time they'd had to have macaroni and cheese for dinner on Thursday because there was a strike at Ford Claycomo and cash was short, every time they had to buy their kids Converses instead of Nikes."

"And Peter Damon is O.J.?" Rep asked.

"Romany Road ain't quite Brentwood, but it looks pretty fancy from Blue Springs or Raytown. Or from anywhere much east of Troost, for that matter. If we just pick holes in the prosecution's evidence and make some noise about Pendleton sending his own boys over to grab the saber, maybe find a few other wives Quinlan rogered so we can put their husbands on trial—that Criminal Law 101 stuff isn't gonna get it."

"The O.J. syndrome is that bad, huh?"

"That bad and worse," Archer said, glancing over at Rep. "Count Basie called Kansas City a happy town. He was right. Our cooking is better than New Orleans', our honest politicians are cleaner than Minnesota's, our crooked politicians are more colorful than Chicago's, and our jazz is better than what passes for blues in St. Louis. But don't let that cheerful attitude fool you. Southern populist working-class resentment is bred in the bone here. It's not just a question of *dealing* with the O.J. syndrome, we've gotta turn it in our favor. We gonna save Peter without putting Linda in the soup, we have to find someone richer than Peter Damon doing something nasty in this story."

"Peter didn't own a DeLorean, for starters," Rep said.

"We're communicating." Archer spun toward Rep and his voice took on the kind of pulpit resonance that Rep imagined juries heard from him. "Turns out what you said before is exactly right. The money pieces *are* the key. This case *reeks* of money. Five-figure checks being thrown around like confetti. Fast cars, fast lives, fast sex. There's a Quinlan-money connection at Jackrabbit Press. There has to be."

"Do you really think it has anything to do with the murder?"

"Doesn't matter what I think," Archer said. "All that matters is what the jury thinks."

"So we have to put some of those puzzle pieces together."

"Right. Get ourselves a plausible dirty-money alternative scenario going and tell the jury, 'We *gave* the police this. We *handed* it to them on a silver platter. But they didn't investigate it because they didn't wanna uncover anything about Mr. Quinlan that might embarrass Massa John Paul Lawrence with his fancy donations and his political pull and his big country house.'"

"Pretty raw," Rep said.

"So is the death penalty."

"*Touché.*"

"It can't just be a clever story with winks and nudges, though. We'll need some honest-to-God, sonofabitchin' *evidence.*"

A light bulb went off over Rep's head. The evidence, if there was any, was at Jackrabbit Press. It wouldn't be there for long. The police wouldn't go after it. Archer couldn't go after it. He couldn't tell Rep to go after it. All he could do was state the obvious and hope Rep had at least as many street smarts as your average white guy.

Saying yes meant crossing a line, as he had when he'd braced Trevelyan—who, now that Rep thought about it, was slow enough for Rep to outrun. That made him a plausible suspect for last night's library shooting. And Rep had no trouble seeing him at a shady midnight meeting with Quinlan. But taking Archer's hint meant more than holding Linda's hand and searching a few databases. If there was nothing at Jackrabbit Press, it meant acting like fools. And if there was something there, it meant going in harm's way.

"If I were you I'd start now," Rep said. "The next thing I've got to do is call Andy Pignatano."

Archer glanced over at Rep for a long moment. Then he nodded. They were on the same page.

"There is the matter of my retainer," he said. *Which I really shouldn't take from Linda until we clear up the little detail of whether I'm going to accuse her of murder.*

"Oh, right," Rep said. "Do you take American Express?"

Archer's eyes opened quite wide. For the first time that morning he seemed on the verge of laughter.

"I have been practicing criminal law twenty-seven years," he said, "and that is the first time that anyone has ever asked me that question."

Chapter 21

"Have you ever taken money or drugs for sex or had sex even one time with anyone who has?"

"No," Linda answered mechanically. Melissa's throat clinched a bit as the young woman in the starched white uniform noted Linda's answer.

"Since 1977 have you traveled to sub-Saharan Africa or had sex even once with anyone who has?"

"Ah, no."

This is a LOT worse than the confessional, Melissa thought. *Adultery isn't for blood donors, at least if they're as scrupulous as Linda.*

"Do you understand that you can be HIV positive and feel fine?"

"Yes."

"Are you donating blood for the purpose of being tested for AIDS?"

"No."

"Do you understand the use of the bar-code?"

"Yes."

"All right, then." The young woman handed Linda the card she had been filling out and a piece of adhesive backing with two bar-code labels on it. One was marked USE MY BLOOD, the other DESTROY MY BLOOD. Then she ostentatiously turned her body away from Linda.

"All right," Linda said a moment later, handing the card back with the USE MY BLOOD bar-code stuck on it and the other disposed of.

Cognitive dissonance, Melissa thought as they got up to go to the couch where Linda's blood would be drawn. The cognitive dissonance assailing her now made the problem she'd mentioned to Linda at the beginning of this misadventure seem like a romp in the park. Trying to believe two contradictory things was hurting her head more than freshman term papers did.

Thing one: Peter didn't do it and neither did Linda.

"Which arm would you like to use?" a different, not so young woman in a starched, white uniform was asking Linda now.

"The left."

"May we see both arms please?" *Just in case you're a needle-drug user.*

"Of course."

But then, Melissa thought, *there's Thing two: the bloody sword.* She had gone over the timing again and again, trying to imagine some way Quinlan could have gotten from the seduction *manqué* of Melissa at his DeLorean to the encampment Port-A-Potty and had his throat cut, with the murderer having time to get back to Jackrabbit Press and replace Peter's saber, all before Peter got downstairs and retrieved the weapon. The conclusion was always the same: *No way.* In honor of Klimchock, in fact, make that, *no bloody way.*

"Please make a fist and squeeze the ball. You'll feel a sting."

A little gasp from Linda as the needle went in. The pain was slight, Melissa knew from her own experience, but she had the feeling that Linda was embracing it, welcoming the physical hurt as a token of atonement. Maybe that instant of pain and the tedium before and after it were why she'd insisted on keeping an appointment any sane person would have cancelled.

Melissa's cell phone rang and she answered it.

"Hello, Nora," Rep said, "this is Nick."

"Developments?" Melissa asked.

"I've gone out on a limb. I called Pignatano and promised him that we could produce Linda at Jackrabbit Press for some in-depth Q and A with him and Lawrence. He's got us penciled in for mid-morning tomorrow. But that's only if you two buy into the concept after we've had a chance to talk. If you don't, I'll call him back and beg off."

"Don't you like Archer?"

"I like Archer a lot," Rep said. "But Pignatano doesn't know that. The Pignatano appointment is basically Archer's idea. At least I *think* it's his idea."

"What exactly is the idea, and why does it involve seeing Pignatano?"

"The idea is to get us inside Jackrabbit Press, and chatting with Pignatano is the only way I can think of to do it."

"In other words," Melissa said after pausing for a moment, "after your very dogmatic lecture, we're going to play Nick and Nora after all?"

"Maybe not Nick and Nora. Maybe just Jerry and Susan North."

"I don't think Jerry and Susan will work," Melissa said. "All the real work in those stories is done by a couple of New York detectives, who tumble to the solution when Susan unwittingly blurts out a key insight in the second-last chapter. Until then all she does is stumble over corpses, and all Jerry does is mix martinis and occasionally light Susan's cigarettes. Given our rather moderate habits, that would leave you with too much idle time."

"Nick and Nora then," Rep said. "But I'll be counting on you for a searing insight even so—a witting one, if possible."

"I'll do my best," Melissa said. "You can pick us up in about an hour, after the donation is complete and Linda has had her juice and cookies. We'll talk things over and figure out what to do next."

"What Linda's going to do next is sit down with Norm Archer and work on a statement for the police, and I'm counting on you to get her back to Archer's shop for that purpose. Because what I'm going to do next is learn anything I can about cases where Pignatano represented Lawrence or Jackrabbit Press. By an hour from now I should have made it to the records room of the federal courthouse here. I'm hoping you can meet me there."

"Count on it," Melissa said. "One hour."

She put the cell phone away and settled back in her molded fiberglass chair, wondering how to stumble over a searing insight. She glanced at Linda, who lay back with her eyes closed, a troubled expression marring her face. Looked at the clear, plastic tube leading from Linda's left arm, tracked the rich flow of blood that Linda's strong, young heart was pumping through it, followed the flow up the tube to the slowly filling plastic bag at the top.

There Melissa's gaze stopped, and her world suddenly took on an exquisite clarity. Every speck of cognitive dissonance evaporated from her psyche. She had seen a Baggie-on-steroids like that before, with thick sides and seals that looked like they meant business. And the guy who'd shown it to her had been a marathon runner.

◇◇◇

"Any luck?" Melissa whispered to Rep fifty-eight minutes later.

"Zilch," Rep said, pushing back in discouragement from the carrel where a desktop computer terminal blinked unhelpfully at him. "All I've established in more than three hundred dollars' worth of non-billable time spent pawing through index cards and doing mouse-clicks in the basements of two courthouses is that neither Jackrabbit Press nor John Paul Lawrence has ever been represented by Andy Pignatano or anyone else in either a civil or a criminal case in the Jackson County Circuit Court or the United States District Court for the Western District of Missouri."

"I read an interesting theory about military policy once," Melissa said. "The author said that the best army in the world isn't the American or the British or the Israeli, despite their outstanding battlefield performances. He said the best army is the Swiss—because it never has to fight."

"You're saying maybe Pignatano is such a good lawyer for Lawrence and Jackrabbit Press that he keeps them out of court."

"Right. After all, don't you keep a lot of your clients out of court?"

"Sure. But I'm a trademark and copyright lawyer. Pignatano is a trial lawyer, specializing in white collar crime and immigration. Trial lawyers get clients by defending them in court. If they impress their clients doing that, they can branch out into other things. But you wouldn't consult Andy Pignatano in the first place unless you had a problem involving people with badges. And a problem like that should show up on a docket somewhere."

"Is there any possibility he's not actually their lawyer?" Melissa asked.

"Not after yesterday's performance. He's not a guy Lawrence talked to for the first time this week after a referral. He did something somewhere along the line to win John Paul Lawrence's complete confidence."

"Will that database you're logged onto sort by lawyer? Maybe you should just bring up all the cases where Pignatano appeared for anyone."

"I don't have any better ideas," Rep shrugged as he complied.

The screen filled with captions and case numbers. A bar at the bottom said that three more screens awaited him when he got through with this one. Hmm. He decided to cheat by looking at the J's and the L's first—a little screenscam that might make the chore less tedious. Melissa bent eagerly over his shoulder and avidly perused the data with him.

The J's turned up nothing useful. *Serves me right*, Rep thought.

"Try the L's," Melissa said.

"You read my mind."

"It's a habit."

He scrolled down impatiently to LAW.

"Looks like Emmett Lawrence had a problem with the Treasury Department back in '99," Melissa said.

"If it was the kind of problem I suspect it was," Rep said, "he should be getting out just about now."

"No John Pauls," Melissa said, "and we're all the way down to Lawton."

Rep began scrolling back up, past Emmett Lawrence.

"Lawless?" Melissa read tentatively.

"Neat name in this context, but no help. Ditto Lawaski."

"And now you're at LAV and LAU."

"Right," Rep said distractedly, an instant before his index finger froze on the mouse. "Bingo. Melissa, my treasure, you are a genius."

"That goes without saying," she said. "But what have you found?"

"André Laurent versus United States Immigration and Naturalization Service," Rep said. "'Laurent,' like Laurent Fabius, the French politician in a story Peter told me on the way to the encampment."

"Of course," Melissa said. "The French version of Lawrence."

"Time to look for hard copy," Rep said, madly scribbling the case number down.

Fifteen minutes later they had a thin and, at first glance, not terribly illuminating file. Although André Laurent had been in the United States for some four decades by 1987, according to a complaint signed by Andrew Pignatano, the INS had designs on deporting him, and was proceeding in a manner that Pignatano found arbitrary, capricious, and inconsistent with most of the Constitution and all of the Administrative Procedure Act.

"But he doesn't say *why* they're trying to deport him," Melissa complained.

"Plead thin and win," Rep acknowledged. "Don't show your cards. *Pro forma* denial from the U.S. Attorney. Routine scheduling order. No discovery motions. No hearings, transcripts, or written decisions. Then the thing is dismissed as moot sixty-eight days after it was filed. Tantalizing but not terribly informative."

"Is it important that this is called a 'verified complaint'?" Melissa asked.

"Might be," Rep said. "I hadn't noticed that. That's something you usually file only if you think you might be running into court right away and need to impress the judge fast."

The verification form at the end of the complaint presented eye-glazing legal boilerplate: "I declare under penalty of perjury that the allegations set forth above are true and correct of my own knowledge, except for those made on information and belief, and as to them I believe them to be true."

This would of course be signed "André Laurent." Except that it wasn't. It was signed "John Paul Lawrence."

"So John Paul Lawrence is an immigrant from France who changed his name from André Laurent?" Melissa speculated.

"Maybe," Rep said. "But in 1947 he couldn't have been more than ten or twelve years old, if that. What could someone that age have done that would interest the INS forty years later, even on a slow day?"

"So we need to beg Diane Klimchock for permission to use the library's vast research resources some more," Melissa said.

"I think we have to ask her to do the Googling herself, if she's game," Rep said. "After last night, the library might be a bit too hot for you and me, unless we want to spend the next six hours being grilled by cops."

"So what are we going to do?"

"Talk about the big picture, while we wait for Linda and Klimchock. And I'd like to do the talking and waiting somewhere that isn't in the shadows of the Kansas City, Missouri Police Department. You have any ideas?"

"Yes," Melissa said, "even though the Kansas City Jazz Museum is out."

Chapter 22

"That's a magnificent piece, isn't it?" Rep commented, nodding at a Qing dynasty painted porcelain vase whose elegant lines suggested a delicate lightness despite its size.

"Try to sound impressed instead of surprised," Melissa said. "Kansas Citians are trained to take umbrage at easterners who come to the Nelson-Adkins Gallery expecting to see nothing but Thomas Hart Benton paintings and a few Remington cowboy sculptures."

"Not guilty," Rep replied with a hint of indignation. "I read the *New York Times.* I would have known that the Nelson-Adkins had a world class collection of Asian art even if Diane Klimchock hadn't mentioned it twice in the first sixty seconds after you told her we'd be here this afternoon."

"You're right, it is lovely," Melissa said. "If we have to be cooling our heels, I suppose this is a great place to do it. But I wish I could be with Linda instead, while she goes through her ordeal with Archer and the police."

Rep glanced at his watch. Almost three thirty.

"She shouldn't be much more than another hour, if Archer's estimate is right," he said.

"Archer also estimated that the police would have found Peter by early this afternoon, but they apparently haven't turned him up yet," Melissa said.

"Yeah, and that surprises me. Nothing in this psycho-drama has been simple, though, so why should finding Peter be any different?"

Melissa stepped forward a couple of feet for a closer look at one of the brass hawks framing the vase. She gazed for a moment at the bird's casually predatory expression.

"Actually," she said, "I'm still convinced that the most important element in this puzzle has to be simple: the thing that triggered Peter's sudden exit from the encampment."

"Maybe," Rep said. "Except that it if it wasn't Linda's tresses tied to a bolt, it's probably something as simple as a hideously complex twist in a revenue bond proposal."

"The underlying issue may be complicated, but the trigger has to be simplicity itself. Peter has just been doing heavy petting with the love of his life and thinks she's hinting at pregnancy. The next thing he knows she's in the bathroom tossing her cookies. Whatever he saw between her dash for the john and his exit interview with you had to nail him right between the eyes, hit him like a thunderbolt. It had to be something that produced an instant epiphany, and convinced him that he had to do something *right now*."

Melissa punctuated the remark with a fist-smack into her left palm emphatic enough to draw a startled glance from a guard in the corner of the hall. Melissa prudently led Rep from the Chinese Furniture Room to the Chinese Scholar's Studio across the hall, where two Han dynasty chimera sculpted almost two thousand years before awaited them.

"The thunderbolt must have related to the library expansion," Rep said.

"Right. But it also had to have something to do with Jackrabbit Press, and probably with Linda. Peter isn't an oaf, and he adores her. Whatever he saw had to be something that he could at least imagine hurting Linda somehow, even if only by association. Something that would make her or someone else think she was a horrible person instead of the faultless angel that he saw her as. Do you think I'm a faultless angel, by the way?"

"No, I'm pretty sure you have free will. And you ended your penultimate sentence with a preposition."

"All right. '...the faultless angel he saw her as, asshole.'"

"You stole that line from Lou Piniella."

"And I did it quite deliberately," Melissa said.

"That makes you seem even wiser to me than you did a week ago—and I would have bet that wasn't possible."

"You're really a dear when you're not correcting my grammar."

"If you're right, the problem is pretty straightforward. All we have to do is figure out what the thunderbolt was."

A third voice intervened before Melissa could respond, which was probably a good thing.

"That's a splendid griffin, isn't it?" the voice said, apparently referring to one of the chimera. "Or is it a dragon?"

Rep and Melissa glanced over their shoulders to see Klimchock, holding a large manila envelope. She seemed to be sedulously avoiding eye contact, as if the three of them were about to execute a dead letter drop in 1968 Prague. "Any news on Peter yet?"

"None that's reached us," Rep said. "I hope that whatever you've learned is worth the drive."

"Rather yes, I think," Klimchock said. "Melissa's last thought about the medal was spot on. During the Nazi occupation of France, Vichy created a decoration called the Francisco, for civilian government officials. You had to be tight with the wrong sort of people even to think about being put up for one."

"No surprise after other things we learned," Rep said, "but still ugly."

"To continue. Lawrence turns out to have been born in Arles, France. The name on his baptismal certificate is J-E-A-N P-A-U-L L-A-U-R-E-N-T. In other words, the fruits of your courthouse search were juicy indeed. Admittedly, as you also pointed out, someone who's sixty-five years old today would have been a bit young for collaborationist activity during World War II. But the same thing cannot necessarily be said about his father."

"Named André, by any chance?" Rep asked.

"Yes. André was born in 1908. Degree from the *École* something-or-other, then into provincial posts in the civil service. Called back to the colors in the run-up to World War II. Served until demob following the debacle in 'forty. Emigrated to this country with his family after the war. Somewhere in between the last two he won himself a Francisco."

"It fits," Melissa said.

"He seems to have had enough of a packet to start a printing business that eventually flourished under John Paul. Died in 1987 of a self-inflicted gunshot wound."

"Which is why the lawsuit suddenly became moot," Rep said.

"You've been busy," Melissa said to Klimchock.

"As I said, Peter and the new wing are top of the list at the moment."

"I think we'd better leave Chinese art and head for pre-Columbian," Rep said.

"All right, I'll bite," Melissa said. "Why?"

"Because it's between here and the coffee shop, and I need something caffeinated."

"Right, then," Klimchock said. "I'm away. Stay in touch."

Twenty minutes later, Rep pushed a glass of Diet Coke across the glass top of a wrought iron table, thoughtfully stuffed sheets back into the envelope, and looked into Melissa's eyes without seeing them.

"Conclusions?" Melissa asked.

"John Paul Lawrence knows more about making money than I do. Beyond that, it's a lot of guesswork. What all those guesses have in common, though, is Jackrabbit Press."

"How about the Civil War battles on the disk Peter left at the library?" Melissa asked. "Have you come up with a theory about why anyone would have that particular set on one disk?"

"No. Spotsylvania and Cold Harbor were the beginning of the attrition phase of the Civil War, grinding Lee's army down by force of numbers. Jubal Early's Valley campaign is famous because Lincoln personally observed some of the fighting, and the future Justice Holmes was wounded. But the only reason I've ever heard anybody even mention the Battle of Cedar Creek is Sheridan's dramatic ride from Winchester to save the day."

"Really?" Melissa said. "That was Sheridan's Ride?"

"Well, yeah," Rep said. "But how do you know about it?"

"'Sheridan's Ride' is a poem by Thomas Buchanan Read," Melissa said. "Wildly popular in the post-Civil War years. 'The terrible grumble, and rumble, and roar/Telling the battle was on once more/And Sheridan twenty miles away.' I can just see roomfuls of schoolgirls memorizing it while Dorothea Dix frowned over them."

"I think you're onto something," Rep said.

"You'd better explain what it is, then."

"The Battle of Cedar Creek wasn't terribly important militarily, but that poem's celebration of the dramatic ride could be used to create interest in it anyway. Cedar Creek could be the scene of a major re-enactment, on the scale of much more famous battles. If nobody is planning a re-enactment right now, it wouldn't take much public relations effort to gin one up."

A game-face look steadily replaced the expression of simple intellectual curiosity on Melissa's face. She caught her husband's eyes and held them.

"We're going to have to do it, aren't we?" she said. "Go out to Jackrabbit Press?" It wasn't really a question and Rep didn't really have to nod to confirm his answer but he did, just as Melissa's cell phone rang.

"That was Linda," she said after a thirty-second chat. "The police are through with her. She can sleep in her own bed tonight. Still no sign of Peter. She wants to meet us at her house."

"Good," Rep said. "Because we have a lot to do before tomorrow morning. Starting with pinning down the date for the Battle of Cedar Creek."

Chapter 23

The sprawling reception room at Jackrabbit Press showed no traces Friday morning of the Civil War setting from Tuesday night. Framed covers of period romances supplemented historical prints and paintings on the walls. A Chesterfield sofa and mate's chairs in matching maroon leather defined a waiting area around a low maple table holding *The New York Times*, *The Kansas City Star*, and a month's worth of *People*.

Lawrence and Pignatano greeted Rep, Melissa, and Linda around nine thirty at Henderson's desk. Henderson smiled briefly at Rep. If Jackrabbit Press had any other employees on site that day, Rep saw no evidence of them. Lawrence pressed Linda's right hand with paternal warmth.

"I know that our loss is your loss as well," he said. (It occurred to Rep that this perhaps wasn't the most tactful phraseology under the circumstances.) "Thomas always said that you were the most talented editor he worked with, and I know how highly you thought of him. At the moment, though, you and Peter have things far more important than manuscripts and production schedules to worry about. If you think legal advice would be helpful, Mr. Pignatano is here to assist in any way he can."

"That's very generous, Mr. Lawrence. I've been wandering around in a daze since Tuesday night. I don't know where to turn."

"Then let's go to the conference room and talk it through, shall we?"

"This will sound silly, but could we talk in the editorial office instead? That's where I worked with Tommy, and I'd feel more comfortable."

"I understand perfectly," Lawrence said, his smile silky and tender at the same time. "Regrettably, however, the police have asked us to stay out of that office for a few more days, in case they want to check it further."

"Mmm, sure," Linda said, nodding. "Conference room, then."

Nice try, but no cigar, Rep thought. *Time for Plan B.*

His right hand in the side pocket of his sport coat, Rep pressed the SEND button on his cell phone. He had punched Melissa's number into the phone just before they entered the building. Six seconds later (for the satellite apparently had other things to do that morning), after they had moved several strides past Henderson's desk, Melissa's phone beeped. She answered the phone while Rep pressed the speaker on his phone as hard as he could against the inside lining of his jacket pocket.

"I can't talk now, I'm about to go into a meeting," Melissa said impatiently. Then a note of urgent alarm crept into her voice. "What, Sheila? Is it about Mom? Just a minute."

Lowering the phone, she looked at the others with an expression combining anxiety with contrition.

"I'm sorry," she said. "You all go ahead. I've got to take this."

Without waiting for reaction, she turned away from them and walked back toward the reception area. She returned the phone to her ear and, head lowered, whispered urgently into it. She continued this pantomime for about two minutes, slumping into one of the mate's chairs, rocking gently back and forth, taking measured breaths as if to calm herself. Then she put the phone down and held it with both hands in her lap as she looked straight ahead.

She resisted the urge to offer Henderson an explanation. She hoped that, left to her own devices, Henderson would work out a better story than Melissa could invent. Doing her best to look worried and then bored, Melissa counted slowly to three hundred.

At that point she opened her purse. It held three things that wouldn't ordinarily have been there, and she now took two of them out: a pack of Virginia Slims, and a book of matches. Tucking her purse under her left arm and raising the cigarettes and matches in her right hand, she turned sheepishly toward Henderson.

"Excuse me," she stage-whispered, "is there a place where I can smoke without bothering anyone?"

"Sure," Henderson said, offering Melissa an I've-been-there smile. "Straight out the back door, on the porch. There's some shade and a place to sit and a butt-can filled with sand. It's not fancy, but it should do."

"Thanks," Melissa said. She rose and headed for the hallway that would take her past the conference room and toward the back door. On the way, she stopped near Henderson's desk. "Please don't tell my husband," she whispered conspiratorially. "I promised him that I'd quit, and I mostly have, but I'm afraid I've relapsed a little this past week."

"Don't worry," Henderson said, giving her a thumbs-up.

Melissa walked down thirty feet of hallway, past the stairs and then the conference room door, to a kitchen that Lawrence had converted into an employee lounge and lunch room. Leading from that room to the back porch was a Dutch door, carefully preserved and clearly intended to look as if someone were actually about to set freshly baked apple pie out to cool on the lower half.

Melissa slipped out of the espadrilles she was wearing. She punched the general number for Jackrabbit Press into her cell phone and rested her right thumb on the SEND button. She pushed the back door open and then pulled it sharply closed, loudly enough for Henderson to hear.

Taking a deep breath, she pushed the SEND button and at the same instant began quietly backtracking. She heard a discreet burr from the reception area, followed by Henderson's polished, professional voice saying, "Jackrabbit Press. How may I direct your call?... Jackrabbit Press.... Hello? Is anyone there?"

By "hello" Melissa had gotten all the way back to the stairway. She began going up, moving as lightly as she could and praying that Henderson's exasperation with the unresponsive caller would cover any stray creaks Melissa produced. She made it unchallenged to the top and for the second time in her life found herself facing, a scant dozen feet away at the end of the upstairs hallway, a solid-looking, thoroughly contemporary mahogany door that announced in raised, pewter letters:

JACKRABBIT PRESS
Editorial Office
R. Thomas Quinlan Imprint

No yellow police tape barred the doorway. Perhaps fifteen feet down the wall from that door was its twin brother, this one marked:

OFFICE OF THE PUBLISHER
John Paul Lawrence

Melissa now took the third unwonted item from her purse: the key to the first door, which Linda had given her. She strode to the door, worked the key laboriously into the lock, turned hard, pushed the door open, and went in.

◇◇◇

He's good, Rep thought as he listened to the gently but insistently probing questions that Pignatano asked in a serenely reassuring, carefully nonthreatening tone.

"The single most helpful thing we could do at this point," Pignatano was saying now, "is figure out where Peter is. That way, we can get him a lawyer he has confidence in—maybe me, maybe Mr. Pennyworth here, maybe someone else—so he can come in to the police and they'll stop looking for him."

"Won't they arrest him?" Linda asked.

"They might, and that won't be any picnic," Pignatano said. "But it's a lot less unpleasant if we're in control of the process. Apart from everything else, if Peter voluntarily appears we have at least an outside shot at getting bail. The very worst thing would be for the cops to find him at a TraveLodge somewhere in western Kansas under an assumed name."

"I can't believe Peter would run away," Linda said.

You probably can't believe he'd carve Tommy Quinlan up like a Halloween pumpkin either, Rep and Pignatano thought simultaneously.

"Well," Pignatano said, "we need to drill down a little deeper into where he could be, then."

"I've racked my brain," Linda said, "I really have."

"I know. I know you've tried to think of every conceivable place. But now let's take that process to the next level. If he were in any of the logical places around Kansas City, the police would certainly have found him by now. We have to get outside the box and really use our imaginations, come up with some possibilities that wouldn't occur to anyone the first time around."

"All right," Linda said, "I'll try. Let me think."

At the end of her eighth belly-churning minute inside the editorial offices, Melissa perched, baffled, on the edge of Quinlan's desk. Sweat pearled her chin and the back of her light blouse stuck to sodden shoulder blades, for the undersized window air conditioner on the other side of the room wasn't on.

She hadn't wasted her time up to now. Under Quinlan's desk she had found a Scotsman mini-refrigerator with a tiny freezer and no ice trays. She had come across a bill from Hickman Mills Medical Laboratory that had apparently arrived with that morning's mail. It demanded $154.75 for "Professional Services" that, according to a box checked on the bottom of the invoice, were NOT COVERED BY INSURANCE. Both suggestive, neither conclusive.

What she hadn't found was the thunderbolt. The thing that had crystallized Peter's thinking and galvanized him into action. She knew that it not only had to be here, but had to be in plain sight. But she couldn't spot it.

She stood up and walked over to the desk that Linda used when she worked at the office instead of at home. Linda had said that when she'd talked to Peter Tuesday night she had started by pulling her desk chair out to one side and parking herself directly opposite the visitor's chair where he'd been sitting. She'd wanted to pour her heart out face to face, without any barrier in between them. Melissa now pulled the visitor's chair away from the desk a bit, angled it, and sat down in it as if she were Peter facing Linda.

She couldn't imagine Peter's eyes anywhere but on Linda as they talked and then clinched and kissed like a couple of teenagers in the back seat of dad's Lexus. She pictured them coming up for air while Peter ecstatically imagined fatherhood and Linda suddenly felt her gorge rising. She mimed Peter stepping back, baffled and anxious, when Linda sputtered her hurried exit line, then Peter turning to watch as Linda hustled out the door.

Then Peter—what? She had no idea. Maybe he'd stood there gaping at the doorway. Maybe he'd wandered randomly around the office, idly fingering paperweights and glancing at the flotsam and jetsam of office life. Maybe he'd picked up a manuscript and scanned a page or two. No matter how systematically Melissa did it, any further reconstruction of his movements would amount to pure conjecture.

She rapped her knuckles on Linda's desk. She had stood in this room herself, Tuesday night, not long after Peter had. Whatever he had seen she must have seen then, without noticing it. She tried to remember the way the room had looked to her that night, how it had seemed different than this morning aside from not being as stiflingly hot and close.

She looked again at the doorway to the hall. Then, quite deliberately, trying now not to reconstruct Peter's movements but to jog her own recollection of the room that night, she racked her head back the other way, five degrees of arc at a time, noting each image that came within her field of vision.

Haphazardly laden bookshelves starting next to the hallway door and following the wall around its inside corner. Remainders, advance-reader copies, and manuscripts spilling onto the floor. Quinlan's large, L-shaped desk in front of the shelves, dominating that quarter of the office. No melodramatic note from Tuttle spiked to his chair this time, but the difference nagging at her went beyond that. A connecting door to Lawrence's office just beyond the bank of shelves. The wall on the other side of that door, most of it taken up by an enormous calendar on erasable whiteboard showing editorial and production schedules for three titles. The intersecting wall along the rear of the building, with its window and non-functioning air conditioner—no wonder it felt so sticky in here. More shelves, canted a bit under the strain of—

Wait. She remembered Tuesday night as also rather warm, but she hadn't felt herself suffocating in this room. She didn't recall hearing the air conditioner. She shifted her eyes back to it. It wasn't just off. It looked disused, somehow, as if it hadn't been on for quite awhile. A naked bolt peeked through where one of the control knobs was missing. She walked over to the machine and flipped the ON button. Nothing. Not even a fan. She returned to her vantage point at Linda's desk.

So what? So…why hadn't this room seemed like a sweltering precursor of Purgatory Tuesday night? She swept her gaze back the other direction—and she had it. The connecting door to Lawrence's office hadn't been closed, as it was now, but ajar. The resulting draft had cooled the room just enough to take the edge off the heat.

She strode across the room. She pushed the connecting door open. And caught the thunderbolt right between her eyes.

Mounted on an easel in front of Lawrence's desk, the painting had to be four feet high by twelve feet long. It depicted a sparkling warship—a destroyer, Melissa guessed, although she certainly wasn't an expert—cutting proudly through a white-flecked, sunlit sea. Large white letters along the prow read U.S.S. LIBERTY.

Even if Tuttle's note hadn't monopolized her attention Tuesday night and she'd noticed the painting, it probably wouldn't have clicked. With the discoveries of the past two days, though, her epiphany was so complete and at the same time so grotesque that it took her breath away. Understanding snapped into place. Not for nothing was she married to a guy who'd gotten his bachelor's degree in twentieth-century history. During the Six Day War in 1967 between Israel and four Arab countries, Israeli warplanes had attacked and severely damaged the *U.S.S. Liberty,* killing several crewmen. Israel had pled that the attack was a tragic error, and the United States had accepted that assurance. The *U.S.S. Liberty* had nonetheless become an icon for some of the more ferocious strains of anti-Semitism lurking in the slimy sub-basement of American life.

The implications appalled her, but a thrill of elation mingled with the disgust. Peter hadn't killed Quinlan. He was innocent. Linda wins, logic loses.

Peter had seen this painting. He had imagined it hanging in the entrance to the Jackson County Public Library extension. He had realized in an instant's insight that Lawrence might be trying to pervert the naming of the new library wing to serve his own bigotry. Maybe he'd wondered if Linda somehow knew about this, felt guilty about it, if that was what had her vomiting her guts up.

But Melissa didn't need to push her theory that far. Peter being Peter, worshiping at the altar of Words, capable of seeing God's hand in well-wrought similes and humble verbal by-play, needed no more than the painting itself to galvanize him. One shattering instant of realization, and Peter would have concluded that the very next thing he had to do was find out whether, buried in the boilerplate of impenetrable legal documents, the official name of what everyone was calling the proposed Liberty Memorial Library Wing was the "*U.S.S. Liberty* Memorial Wing." Because if that was what was going on, Klimchock had to be warned not to send Peter's name to the Finance Committee first thing the following morning. That was why Peter had run off. And Melissa knew with apodictic certainty that he hadn't paused for some triviality like killing Quinlan on the way.

Okay, ladies, she thought, *mission accomplished. Exit, stage rear.*

Melissa scurried out of Lawrence's office and pulled the door closed behind her. She hustled toward the door from the editorial offices to the hallway. She reminded herself to keep under control, to open the door slowly so as not to attract attention. In the depths of her superego, though, a panicky, guilt-ridden, plaid-skirted schoolgirl with Ripple on her breath was screaming, *Get out of here!* She jerked the door open.

She had time to see the bearded, expressionless man in the blue uniform who was waiting outside, and time to notice the large Remington revolver he was holding at his side. She had time to read the unsurprised and indifferent eyes of someone who knew his business and was in no particular hurry.

What she didn't have time to do was scream. She opened her mouth to yell, but before the first well-rounded decibel could form in her throat the man stuffed a large, bunched, woolen sock deep into her mouth.

Choking and furious, Melissa stepped backward, preparing to turn and run toward Lawrence's office. The man shook his head, once, unconcerned.

She spun on the ball of her right foot. A lancing pain shot through her left arm as the man seized it with his left hand. Effortlessly he crab-walked her toward Linda's desk and pushed her roughly into Linda's chair. She barked her right thigh painfully on the front edge of the seat and her ribs on the top of the chairback as she slammed into the seat.

Looking up, wide-eyed, Melissa saw the man raise his left hand above his right shoulder. Saw the sweaty, hirsute knuckles on the back of the hand. Saw from his face that he did this not in anger, not impulsively, but with the indifferent efficiency of a natural force, like a cold front scattering children at play as it moves through an autumn afternoon. Saw that he wondered whether she'd gotten the message. And without meaning to or thinking about it, told him with her eyes that she had.

Chapter 24

Rep, at roughly this point, was taking off his glasses and rubbing the bridge of his nose. This was a pre-arranged signal, and he prayed Linda would pick it up. She did.

"I just thought of something that might help, but it's a very difficult part of the story for me," Linda said. "What happened between Tommy and me is something I'm still trying to come to terms with. There are times when I can't even believe I did it. I hate to seem wimpy, but Rep, would you mind stepping outside for a few minutes?"

Perfect. Murmuring "Of course" he stood up and moved toward the conference room door.

"Most certainly," Lawrence said at the same time, rising instantly in his turn. "We'll both go. What you say will be for Mr. Pignatano's ears alone."

Nuts, Rep thought. They hadn't anticipated this snag when they'd worked out today's plan. He'd have to improvise. Hobbling a bit on his still tender ankle, he walked Lawrence into the hallway and headed for the reception area, doing his best to look like a husband who expected to see his wife there. He tried to show mild surprise—not shock, not overdoing it—when he didn't.

"Excuse me," he said to Henderson, "do you know where my wife went?"

"Ladies room?" Henderson said uncertainly. "She had to step away."

"Well," Lawrence said, "when she comes back please tell her that Mr. Pennyworth and I are waiting for her in my office upstairs. Mrs. Damon wants to be alone for the moment with counsel."

"Certainly, Mr. Lawrence."

Alarm bells rang shrilly in Rep's head. In one sentence he had lost control of the situation and he didn't know what to do about it. The plan was to use the Linda/Pignatano chat Lawrence wanted as cover for a search of Jackrabbit Press. Now, all of a sudden, Rep felt like the one being gamed. Lawrence had the initiative; Rep was reacting. He could turn and run right now, but he wasn't going to leave Linda and Melissa alone in this building. Lacking any better ideas, he followed Lawrence upstairs.

"Is your father still alive, Mr. Pennyworth?" Lawrence asked, glancing over his shoulder at Rep.

Worse and worse.

"No. Dad died when I was sixteen."

"I am sorry to hear it. It's devastating to lose a parent before his time."

"'Before his time' would be debatable in Dad's case," Rep said. "He died of forty Camels and six cans of beer a day plus forty-odd thousand miles a year on the road. Those are choices."

"He wasn't your hero, then?" Lawrence asked as he opened his office door and gestured for Rep to enter.

"When he died I thought Dad was a loser," Rep said. "After I got a little older, I realized that sometimes just getting out of bed and going to work in the morning can be heroic."

"An insight worthy of Saul Bellow at his very best," Lawrence said. He strode over to a highly polished Empire desk in the center of the room and nodded toward the canvas in front of it. "What do you think of the painting?"

Rep, who had hung just inside the door, now walked over to look at the artwork. He'd had a lot of practice keeping his face straight, but he didn't quite manage it now. A smile played across Lawrence's lips.

"Hung in the conference room downstairs," Rep said evenly, "I'd call it an eccentric curiosity that's not to my taste. Decorating the main entrance to the Liberty Memorial Wing of the Jackson County Public Library, it would be an abuse of history."

"Correction," Lawrence said. "The *U.S.S. Liberty* Memorial Wing. Three letters buried in fine print that no one has noticed—and no one will."

"Except Peter."

"A pity, but unimportant. Don't you think the brave American sailors who gave their lives on June 8, 1967 should be remembered?"

"I certainly do. But they shouldn't have their memory hijacked to serve a racist agenda."

"Why is the agenda racist—because our sailors were murdered by Jews instead of Arabs?"

"Israel was fighting for its life in 'sixty-seven against enemies that could attack across every land border it had. Bad things happen in war. Israeli planes attacked the *U.S.S. Liberty* by mistake. That isn't murder."

"Mistake?" Lawrence scoffed. "None of the Arab states had any navy to speak of, or a warship anywhere close to the *Liberty* in size or profile."

"The Soviet Mediterranean Fleet had ships in that category, and they weren't above sailing under false colors," Rep said. "Egypt had supply ships that big, and tapes of radio messages from the Israeli fighters that were released a while back showed they thought that's what they were attacking."

"A Zionist construct," Lawrence shrugged.

"I earn my living in the real world," Rep said. "Down here on Planet Earth, a horrible mistake in the fog of battle makes a lot more sense than Israel deliberately attacking a vessel of its one indispensable ally."

"Unless it was the one ally that would let Israel get away with anything," Lawrence said, affecting a condescending smirk.

Time to cut the nonsense, Rep thought. Lawrence was playing with him. He knew what was going on and Rep didn't. Rep needed to make Lawrence blow a fuse, lose a bit of the control he was effortlessly exercising.

"That painting is an unforced error," Rep said. "Like General Order Number 11 and the Brassilach picture and that medal. It's not enough for you to pursue your vendetta, you have to flaunt what you're doing, rub people's noses in it, and then laugh at them for being too dumb to pick up your clever subtleties. Sooner or later, though, someone was bound to."

"The things you mention are certainly unforced," Lawrence said smugly, showing no sign at all of provocation. "Whether they are errors remains to be seen. So far they don't seem to have cost me anything."

"You're wrong. Some reckless questions I asked made a pilfering sutler think you might have Civil War collectibles lying around, and he snuck up here to see. You were afraid he might come across evidence that you're the one who killed Quinlan—like remnants of blood-soaked clothing that you burned in one of the outbuildings afterward, for example—and you ran him off with a warning shot. You snuck into the library downtown to see if you could find out how much Peter had told Klimchock. You only escaped by firing another shot. Live ammunition twice in one day doesn't suggest a smoothly functioning plan."

"It is functioning well enough to get three people I'm interested in under my control," Lawrence said.

"I think you've actually gone over the edge," Rep said, shaking his head as he decided to play his most provocative card. "Look, I'm sorry your father died before he should have. If you want to build a private shrine to him, go ahead, and if you want to blame the Jews for it I can't stop you. But public libraries are sacred places. You don't have a right to turn one into a monument to bigotry just so you can bury the ghost of a dead collaborator."

The calculated insult fell short of his hopes. Lawrence stiffened and recoiled, but then quickly recovered.

"'Collaborator,'" he said contemptuously. "My father was a *bureaucrat.* A pathetic, paper-shuffling, pencil-pushing clerk. He took forms from his in-box, centered them on his green baize desktop, scribbled his initials on them, stamped them with a red *tampon*, and handed them to a *huissier* to pass on to the *fonctionnaire* two offices down."

"Right," Rep said. "And he did this with enough zeal to get a medal for it. Because some of those forms said, 'Arrest the Jew so-and-so and his family and hold them for deportation to such-and-such labor camp.'"

"No doubt," Lawrence said. "And if he had high-mindedly refused to stamp them, some other glorified clerk would have stamped them in his place. He would have accomplished nothing but to sacrifice food and shelter for himself and his family in a crisis situation."

"Did he accept a few thousand francs or the odd collection of family jewels in exchange for losing a form now and then?" Rep asked. "Is that where the civil servant got the stake he needed to bribe his way into the United States after the war and start a printing business once he got here?"

"Whatever he did, it didn't deserve the death penalty," Lawrence said, his speech getting a little faster and less polished, a bit of the icy control finally slipping. "There was no reason to rake all that muck up decades after it happened, threaten him with deportation in the twilight of his life because some Jew who stumbled over him wanted to settle scores."

The final comments connected the last of the dots, explaining how the deportation proceedings against André Laurent had started. They also removed all doubt about Rep's present situation. Lawrence wouldn't have told Rep this much unless he planned on Rep, Melissa, and Linda ending up dead.

Rep saw no reason to cooperate. He jerked his head and upper body toward the hallway door. Raising a Starr Arms revolver that he grabbed from the desk drawer, the older man moved sideways to block Rep's path.

Rep spun around and hustled for the other door, leading to the editorial offices. *He can't shoot*, Rep told himself, *or I'd be dead already. Even if he could hide my body, gunfire inside the building would be hard to explain to Pignatano and Henderson, who probably aren't in on anything illegal.*

He was right. He reached the door without the white hot explosion inside his head that would signal his brains being spattered all over Lawrence's elegant wainscoting. Throwing the door open, he dashed into the other office.

He saw Melissa in Linda's desk chair. Mouth gagged, hands tied behind her, eyes defiant and now widening in alarm. He saw the bearded man in the blue uniform. He didn't see the other uniformed man against the wall next to the door, and so the searing pain from a metallic smash to the back of his head and the inky blackness that followed came as a complete and thoroughly unpleasant surprise. His last conscious thought was *You total schmuck.*

When Rep groggily shook himself to consciousness a few minutes later, he was bound and gagged in a chair next to Melissa's. Lawrence was on the phone in his adjoining office. Though it made his temples throb to do so, Rep concentrated on picking up Lawrence's words through the still open doorway.

"Yes, Karin, please tell Mr. Pignatano that I don't want to take up any more of his time. He can leave a debriefing on my voice-mail while he's driving back downtown. Mr. and Mrs. Pennyworth are waiting up in my office for Linda. As soon as Mr. Pignatano is on his way you can leave for lunch if you wish, and if you'd like to take an extra hour or so to watch the target-shooting competition at the encampment I don't think that will do any harm."

Rep convulsively jerked his body in an effort to tip over the chair he was tied to. He wanted to make enough noise to alarm Henderson. He got the chair's two left legs a couple of inches off the floor before one of the uniformed guys grabbed Rep's hair and jerked in the opposite direction.

Lawrence glanced at the action, murmured something else into the phone, and hung up. Then he closed the connecting door.

Hearing Linda's steps a minute or so later on the stairs and then in the hallway outside, Melissa felt as if she were watching a slasher flick. Impotently screaming "DON'T!" in her mind at the coed about to open the fatal door, after several of her friends had already made the same mistake.

Three more minutes passed after the footsteps stopped. Rep could hear occasional sounds—a scrape of shoe-sole on parquet, a snatch of human voice—but he couldn't make out any words. Finally, the connecting door opened and Linda walked in.

She shrieked.

Well naturally, Rep thought, *she would scream, wouldn't she?*

"Yell as loudly you wish," Lawrence said. "While we were chatting just now I watched both Pignatano and Karin drive off. There's no one to hear you. If you will stop screaming, however, I will take the gags off your two friends."

Linda choked back what had all the earmarks of a very promising follow-up yelp. Lawrence nodded to his two henchmen, who ungently ripped off the adhesive tape sealing in the socks that had silenced Rep and Melissa.

Rep shook his head and gulped breath. His diaphragm felt hollow. His lungs burned. Gasps, ragged and uncontrolled, escaped from him. Five agonizing seconds later he trusted himself to speak.

"I assume he took the gags off because he wants us to tell him what we know," he said to Melissa. He tried for a conversational tone and, somewhat to his surprise, just about made it.

"He's also worried about autopsies finding aspirated fibers in our lungs," Melissa said, as if they were debating the comparative merits of quiche and subs. "Eleanor Taylor Bland's procedurals are very good on that."

"You're hardly in a position to be flippant," Lawrence said. "Your situation at the moment is not entirely hopeless. I want to keep you alive for awhile yet, and it's in your interest to humor me."

"Until you've got your hands on Peter, you mean," Melissa said.

"If you like. The point is, as long as you're alive you can pray for a miracle. Prayer is a low-percentage tactic, but it's better than nothing. Since you have something to lose, you should avoid undue annoyance."

"If all we have to lose is a long lunch-hour with our hands tied behind us," Rep said, "you can probably bet against complaisance."

"I can't count on coming up with Peter quite that quickly," Lawrence said. "There's a silo—an actual silo, for storing grain, quaint Americana at its tackiest—a few hundred yards west of this building. It's empty. After you give me the information I want, we're going to take you to that silo and keep you there until Peter turns up—unless you provoke me into premature unpleasantness in the meantime."

Another unforced error, Rep thought when he heard the word "silo."

"I wouldn't plan on Peter turning up," Melissa said.

"Oh, he'll be found," Lawrence answered. "He is guileless. I think the reason he hasn't been found already is that the police can't ask questions quite as aggressively as the men working for me can. With the help of the information Linda was kind enough to provide, several gentlemen like the two you have encountered this afternoon, less conspicuously dressed but just as efficient, will be looking for him. If the police find him first, Mr. Pignatano will try to arrange bail. Either way, he'll be out here sooner or later."

"So that you can make it look like Peter killed us," Linda said.

"More or less. What I have in mind, if it's any comfort, is some kind of ghastly accident taking place while he was committing suicide and the rest of you were trying to dissuade him. The black powder used in Civil War-era ammunition is notoriously volatile, and the police will discover that several barrels of it were stored in the silo. It isn't there now, of course, but it will be when the time comes. A dramatic gesture on Peter's part, a stray shot or spark and—BANG!—instant human silage."

"You're banking on no cops looking beyond the obvious," Rep said. "I think the police here are a lot smarter than you think they are."

"The solution to Quinlan's murder that I'll offer them will be simple and straightforward," Lawrence said serenely. "They'll accept the obvious answer."

"What if Peter isn't let out on bail?" Linda asked.

"Then we'll have to come up with a pure accident. It's the kind of thing that can happen when three rank amateurs meddle in a police matter and arrange to meet a fugitive at a silo they didn't know was being used to store explosive material. Ms. Pennyworth apparently brought cigarettes with her. Perhaps we'll work something about careless use of smoking materials into it."

"So as long as Peter is missing, you can't kill us," Linda said.

"'Can't' is the wrong word. I'd prefer not to kill you until the Peter issue is resolved, but if I have to kill you I can and I will. Heroics while you're being taken to the silo, for example, will be both pointless and painful. The target-shooting competition will be going on at the encampment. No one will notice three stray shots less than a mile away. All you'll accomplish is to throw away the slight chance you have."

Lawrence paused and looked at the three of them in turn.

"Now for the part about telling me everything you know," he said.

Chapter 25

"Are we going to tell him everything we know, dear?" Melissa asked Rep with what might have been taken for mild interest.

"Of course. Do you think I want those knuckle-draggers to beat me up?"

Both of the blue-uniformed goons bristled at this and one of them took a step toward Rep. Lawrence grabbed the man's sleeve.

"Mr. Pennyworth is deliberately trying to provoke you," he said. "He wants you to bruise him in a way that the explosion we're planning won't explain, so that the police won't buy the Peter-did-it story."

"Well," Rep said modestly, "it was worth a try."

"Just talk," Lawrence said. "Time is short. If need be, I'm willing to take my chances on the explosion covering all injuries. And if one of you has to be hurt, Mr. Pennyworth, you won't be the first."

"Since you put it that way," Melissa said, "the first thing we know is how you framed Peter for Quinlan's murder."

"Do we know that?" Rep asked.

"Oh, yeah, I haven't had a chance to tell you, but I pretty much confirmed my theory up here."

"The marathon thing?" Rep asked.

"Right," Melissa said. "The reason Quinlan had those super Baggies to keep his pot in is that he bought hospital quality seral fluid bags for his own blood. He had his blood drawn and he kept it here, frozen, so that he could have it reinfused just before a qualifying race. It's called blood doping."

"Wow," Rep said. "You nailed all that down up here?"

"Mm-hmm. He'd shown me one of the Baggies when he was trying to impress me with his stash, and I found the freezer and a lab bill up here."

"Okay," Rep said, nodding and then turning his eyes toward Lawrence. "So what you did was take a bag of Quinlan's own blood from his own freezer and drench Peter's saber with it during the encampment social."

"Then you wiped it off," Melissa interjected, "so Peter wouldn't notice it after you returned the saber to the rack. Which you'd sharpened while you were at it. The saber, not the rack. But you knew that even though you'd wiped the saber off, enough residue to be spotted by a competent forensic chemist would soak into the blade."

"After you killed Quinlan with a similar saber," Rep added, "you hinted to the police about rumors of an affair and Peter's supposed pathological jealousy. The blood on Peter's saber would make him the obvious suspect."

"He's certainly played the role to perfection so far," Lawrence said, smiling. "But I hope you know more than that, because what I've heard up to now is of more interest to Linda than to me."

"I knew Peter couldn't have done it," Linda said.

"You're right," Lawrence said, "he couldn't. Cutting a man's throat takes courage—something Peter conspicuously lacks. Now, continue."

"Well," Rep said, "the first one is hard to top, but another thing we've figured out is why you killed Quinlan."

"Namely," Melissa said, "because he was blackmailing you about using Jackrabbit Press as a front to funnel radical Islamic money into this country to finance long-term terrorist projects in the United States. By the way, as long as you have us under control, would you mind untying me? I'm *not* into bondage, and my wrists are getting stiff."

"The restraints are an unfortunate but prudent necessity," Lawrence said. "Tell me more about the terrorist money."

"That part was pretty plain, once we dug into it," Rep said. "No small press publisher could make enough from genre fiction to support the kind of numbers you're running here. You supposedly benefit from this secondary printing and distribution business, but that business only has three real customers—and they all happen to be offshore, in countries with strong radical Islamic movements."

"Countries where they could buy the same services without ever sending a wire transfer overseas," Melissa said. "Quinlan found out about it."

"Which is how he got the DeLorean," Rep said.

"And how he got his own imprint despite being considerably south of Ruth Cavin on the superstar editor scale," Melissa said.

"And how he got his throat sliced open Tuesday night," Rep said.

Rep looked carefully at Lawrence to gauge his reaction. His face showed clear interest and some surprise, but not shock.

"You see the point, don't you?" Rep said.

"If the point is that you two are too smart for your own good I certainly do see it," Lawrence said.

"Just the opposite," Rep said. "If bumbling interlopers like us can figure this stuff out, the FBI won't have any trouble with it. One corpse could be bad luck. When bodies start piling up like rejection notices from the *New Yorker*, the Feds are going to ask questions no matter how clever you think your set-up is. This operation of yours is blown. Time to cut your losses."

"Thanks for the advice, but I'll take my chances," Lawrence said.

"Bad idea," Rep said. "Because there's one more thing we've learned."

"Don't keep me in suspense," Lawrence said.

Well, Rep thought, *there are bluffs and then there are REAL bluffs.*

"The Battle of Cedar Creek," Rep said. "October 19, 1864."

"What?" Lawrence snapped. There was no mistaking the reaction. That one had hit a nerve.

"The one-hundred-fortieth anniversary of the once-famous Battle of Cedar Creek will be about two weeks before a presidential election," Rep said. "The incumbent candidate in that election will be running on what a great job he's done stopping terrorism and keeping American safe. A major re-enactment of the battle could bring more than a thousand well-armed men within striking distance of Washington, D.C."

"And a few dozen or more of those men will be part of the ersatz Civil War re-enactors' unit Jackrabbit Press is funding," Melissa said. "With untraceable repeating rifles that there's no record of anyone ever buying."

"Twenty of them armed with Spencer carbines and a Civil War field piece modified to handle rocket-propelled grenades could mount an attack in Washington, D.C. that would make the current anti-terrorism policy look like a joke," Rep said.

"And change a presidential election," Melissa said.

"Which is what the people sending you those subsidies have been planning for years," Rep said. "Isn't it?"

Silence floated in the room for several seconds. Lawrence looked coolly from Rep to Melissa and then over to Linda, who seemed oddly calm. Now that she knew Peter's innocence could be proven, it seemed, details like imminent peril to her own life lost importance.

"Well," Lawrence said, "I'm rather glad the professionals, as you call them, won't be having your help in their endeavors."

"Oh they most certainly will have it," Rep said, "unless I make a phone call by five o'clock this afternoon."

Lawrence thought for a moment, then shook his head decisively.

"B movie stuff," he said, looking at his watch. "No sale. You're bluffing."

"If I am," Rep said, smiling maliciously at the two goons, "they won't come. But if I'm not, they will."

Chapter 26

Sometime around four thirty that afternoon, as he shifted for the eight- or nine-hundredth time to relieve the stiffness in his butt produced by sitting on the clammy, concrete floor of the silo, Rep realized that he was ready to die. Not that he *expected* to die anytime soon. Ever since one of the goons had opened the garage-type silo door and Rep had felt the rush of fetid, gassy, foul-smelling air from inside—a quick puff he'd been praying for ever since Lawrence had first mentioned the silo—he'd figured they had at least a fifty-fifty chance of pulling through this scrape.

If the end did come in two or three or four hours, though, he felt that it wouldn't have been a bad life and that he could accept its end without self-pity. He'd done what he wanted to do and had fun doing it. He'd eaten savory food, tasted rich wine, heard beautiful music, seen exquisite art, and said things clever enough to make Melissa laugh. He'd managed a handful of professional triumphs that left him with a feeling of modest pride. He'd finally appreciated his father, and he'd found out who his mother was. He'd shared passionate love with a good woman. If it turned out that death had an appointment with him tonight—well, he'd have died with his face to the enemy, trying to help a friend out of a tight spot. Not a bad life. And not a bad way to end it.

Rep, Melissa, and Linda were sitting in roughly the middle of the silo floor, within the weak circle of illumination cast by a large, battery powered campground light. Their hands were still tied behind them. In the darkness near the door a guard was either sitting or standing—Rep couldn't tell which. Rep tried to shake off some of the sweat streaming from his forehead.

"Must be getting close to five o'clock," he said. "It won't be too much longer now. Couple of hours maybe."

"Do you think they'll get here before Lawrence finds Peter?" Melissa asked, picking up the cue.

"Lawrence isn't going to find Peter." Rep offered this part of the bluff with perfect sincerity, for he now had a pretty good idea of where Peter was, and if that idea was right Lawrence wasn't going to come close to grabbing him. "The interesting question is whether Lawrence will wait around to be arrested or is already on his way to Yemen, or wherever he plans on running off to."

"Shut up," the guard's accented voice ordered from the darkness.

"Just remember one thing," Rep said to the guard in what he hoped was a friendly tone. "If they come in from the top of the silo, that'll mean they've already taken care of any buddies you have outside. It's up to you, but you might want to get out while the getting's good."

Rep didn't notice the guard's muttered response because a thrill shot through him as he felt a slight reduction in the heat inside the silo. Even in high summer in Kansas City the sun eventually got lower in the sky, and the temperature gradually dropped as it did so. This was a matter of some importance to Rep—you might even say a matter of life and death—because what they were sitting in wasn't just a silo. It was a Harvestore®—produced under that registered and very valuable trademark of Engineered Storage Products Company. Rep happened to know a good deal about it.

If this were a made-for-TV movie, of course, he wouldn't be worrying about the temperature. He would have found a conveniently jagged bolt to shred the rope binding his wrists. Then he would have overcome the guard with a bit of derring-do. After that he would have discovered cracks and crevices in the silo's inside wall and used them to climb his way tortuously to the top, whence he could escape down the outside ladder and then rescue the ladies with some more he-man stuff on the outside.

Harvestores®, however, don't have jagged bolts or cracks and crevices. Like all silos, Harvestores® are filled from the top. The freshly harvested grain has to go down with as little impediment as possible. The inside walls of a Harvestore® are molten glass, bolted inside steel skin—and the specially engineered bolts have smooth, rounded heads on the inside.

"I figure they'll search the house first," Rep said after he'd counted off another ten minutes. "They won't know about the silo, of course, but if Lawrence has been insane enough to hang around it'll all be over very quickly anyway. They'll crack him like an egg. Even if he's cut and run, it won't take them long to notice this thing."

"Shut up," the guard said. He didn't say it angrily this time. His voice sounded a bit distracted, as if he were thinking of something else.

"How long did they tell you you'd have to stay here before they relieved you?" Rep asked.

The answer was a vulgarity, offered in a tired, for-the-record tone.

Most Americans probably have the image of silos that Lawrence had expressed: simple, phallic-shaped storage units quaintly evocative of uncomplicated rustic life. Rep had never plowed a furrow or slopped a hog, but he knew how far short of reality this simplistic stereotype fell. A well-made, well-designed silo like the Harvestore® is actually a piece of elegantly complex machinery. It doesn't just store harvested grain. It converts that grain into something more useful, called silage. It does this in part by letting the stored grain generate certain gases which accumulate and then act on the grain.

These gases, unfortunately, also produce heat. Unless you vent the heat, full silos have a nasty habit of exploding, killing or maiming people in the vicinity. If you do vent some of the heated gas, though, then the silo sucks in air, exactly like a pair of lungs inhaling after an expulsion of breath. Fresh air dilutes the gases, leading to loss of silage.

The clever engineers who designed the Harvestore® had solved this problem. Their solution sat up there near the silo's ceiling, invisible in the darkness. It was called Breather Bags®—another registered trademark. Breather Bags® are basically specially designed plastic sacks that Gargantua might have used if he'd done Paul Bunyan's yard work. In the heat of the day, these bags deflate. As the sun goes down, though, and hot gas vents through openings put in the silo's side for that purpose, the air being sucked into the silo through its top goes into these bags, inflating them. The bags hold the air, keeping it from diluting the gases lower in the silo.

Rep was playing head-games with the guard because he hoped the Breather Bags® in this silo would inflate the way they were supposed to as the temperature fell. That is, he was counting on the guys who put this silo together—the salt-of-the-earth sons of toil with short necks and strong backs who watched wrestling on television and bullied people they thought would back down and called Marlboro Lights "slut butts" when they bought them for their girlfriends, those guys—having done the job right.

Another fifteen minutes—or, at least, another nine hundred deliberate second-counts in Rep's head—went by.

"I was just thinking of *The Maltese Falcon*," Melissa said.

"Sure," Rep said, picking up her cue in turn. Having limited himself to relatively simple wagers, he'd always wondered what "six-two-and-even" meant. He raised his voice slightly. "Six-two-and-even they're selling you out, pal," he said, echoing Sam Spade for the guard's benefit.

Rapid bootfalls on concrete. Visible in the pale light from roughly the waist down, the guard bolted into sight. Rep turned his head and hunched just in time to catch the boot's sole and heel on his left shoulder and cheek instead of on his nose and mouth. A high-pitched groan escaped from him as he toppled backward over his bound hands.

"Stop that, you bastard!" Melissa yelled furiously.

"Bitch!" the guard spat, whirling on Melissa.

"Don't!" Linda screamed.

"No!" Rep yelled, trying to warn Melissa.

Swishh-WHOOP! A quickening rustle and then a dull, emphatic thud from the top of the silo.

"Yes!" Rep yelped triumphantly—or as triumphantly as his undignified position allowed. "What'd I tell you? Here they are!"

The guard checked his incipient assault on Melissa and snapped his neck upward. Bending urgently, he grabbed for the campground light. Fumbled it once, got it, turned its pale beam toward the ceiling.

"Down here!" Rep yelled. "He has a gun!"

Swish-WHOOP! Swish-WHOOP!

The guard dropped the flashlight, raised his carbine and pumped four panicky shots toward the ceiling.

POP-HISSSS!

"Gas!" Rep yelled. "Close your eyes and push your faces against the ground!"

Having said this, he didn't do it but waited for a moment, looking at what he could see of the guard. The man took two uncertain steps backward.

"Watch it!" Rep yelled then. "There's an outside door down here!"

The guard turned and ran into the darkness toward the silo's perimeter. Rep tried to roll to his feet, but his head spun and he fell back. The kick had hit him harder than he'd realized. He closed his eyes tightly.

"Control panel, right outside the door," he whispered in Melissa's general direction.

She had already made it to her feet, scraping her knees and tearing her dress in the process. She saw a rectangle of light appear. The guard had opened the door. Hands still bound behind her, she moved toward it cautiously at first, as she saw the guard's bulk blot out much of the light, and then more quickly when he had cleared the doorway.

The center of the doorway led to what looked like a hard rubber bridge that sloped toward the ground. On either side of it a concrete sill about two feet wide ran around the silo. The guard hadn't high-tailed it, as Rep clearly had hoped he would. He had run onto the bridge and stopped. Now he was standing there uncertainly, gazing in apparent confusion at the top of the silo.

Melissa didn't want to step through the doorway more than she hadn't wanted to do anything before in her life. The pains in her arm and thigh and ribs from the goon's manhandling of her hours before still seared her memory. But the bottom of the door was over her head, and she didn't think she could pull it down with her chin or her teeth. Gulping hard, she stepped out onto the concrete sill and looked for the control panel.

It was hard to miss. Eighteen inches square and mounted at eye level on the side of the silo, it stared her in the face the moment she made it onto the sill. Three very healthy-looking, silver dollar-sized push-buttons defined a row down its center. One of them, presumably, would close the door and, if God was watching and in a good mood that day, close it slowly enough for Melissa to get back inside but too quickly for the guard to follow her.

From the corner of her eye she could see the guard turning toward her and raising his carbine. She didn't have time to read whatever lettering was beside each button. She just closed her eyes and banged the top button as hard as she could with her forehead.

"Ouch!" she squealed. "Dammit that hurts!"

This rare vulgarity was lost in the most ungodly racket she had ever heard. It sounded as if every demon in Hell had picked that moment to recreate the tortures of the damned on top of the silo. She didn't know it, but she had pushed the button opening the roof. Gears unlubricated for years screeched in protest as their teeth engaged. Metal left without paint or upkeep sheared against metal exposed to rain and sun and ice in brutal cycles.

This got the guard's attention. He wheeled back to look at the roof, raised his carbine, and squeezed off three more shots.

Melissa was already picking out another button—the bottom one, this time. Bracing herself mentally, she readied her forehead for another collision with whatever industrial-strength material these things were made of. She sensed the guard turning back toward her, leveling his carbine at her.

She snapped her head again.

"Ouch!"

Click! Civil War-era Spencer carbines hold seven cartridges in their magazines, and the guard had already fired seven shots. Which meant that now he'd be reaching for his revolver.

SCREEECH! Metal on metal again, this time a few inches from her. Gears engaged, wheels turned, and the rubber bridge started to move.

It was a conveyor belt, there to carry tons of silage from the silo to waiting trucks. It was neither fast nor intrinsically dangerous. When it was actually doing what it was there to do, farm workers would step onto it and off of it routinely to sweep or shovel out snags here and there.

But it's best to be ready when something under your feet starts moving, and the guard wasn't. With a loud yelp he lost his footing and tumbled onto his back. Arms flailing as the belt moved him toward the ground, he kicked his legs in an effort to turn himself over. As Melissa watched in horror, one of the gears lurking beneath the far edge of the belt caught the ample cuff of the guard's uniform pants. His foot and then the lower half of his leg were pulled inexorably into the moving wheels. Face contorted in unalloyed terror, the guard unloosed a shriek that would have shamed every banshee in Ireland.

If I were as bloody-minded as I ought to be I'd let him go, Melissa thought. But she wasn't and she didn't. She head-banged the bottom button again.

The machine stopped, whether because of what she'd done or because the mangled flesh inside it was more than it could handle she couldn't tell. It was already too late for the guard, though. Three sinister mini-geysers of blood spurted at two- or three-second intervals from the distorted opening that now gaped between the edge of the bridge and its track, and then stopped. The guard's head was thrown back, his silent mouth gaping, his eyes open but sightless. The grisly trauma, lasting perhaps five seconds, had burst his heart.

This was the first time in her life that Melissa had ever seriously hurt another human being, but she decided to save philosophical reflections for later. She ducked back into the silo.

"All right," she said breathlessly, "the guard is dead and I didn't see any others outside."

"Good girl," Rep said.

"Let's go," Linda squealed.

"No," Rep said, "let's stay here. That racket is going to draw a crowd fast, and this will be the last place they'll look."

"Right," Melissa said.

The three of them huddled in the darkest part of the silo they could find. Melissa and Rep stood back-to-back so that Melissa could try to untie Rep's hands. Actors in the endless run of Fifties and Sixties TV westerns that Melissa had watched while she was earning an A in *The Male Hero Construct in Post-War American Popular Culture* had repeatedly done this trick with admirable efficiency and adroitness. Often, they'd start at the commercial break and be done the moment the commercials were over. Melissa found the task considerably more daunting.

"Maybe I should try untying yours," Rep said. "Are your fingernails getting in the way?"

"Not anymore," Melissa said. "They're all gone."

"Shhh!" Linda said. "Someone's coming!"

They all shut up. They all stopped moving. For that matter, they almost stopped breathing. Within a few seconds, a confused hubbub of voices reached them through the door. At first they could only pick up snatches, some of it in a language they didn't understand.

"Look at Lou! How did they manage that?"

"What the—"

"Hey—"

Then Lawrence's voice cut through the chatter. His tone was concerned but calm and clear.

"All right. He still has both guns and we heard the last shots less than four minutes ago, so they can't have gotten far. They're probably headed for the encampment. Twelve of you fan out and look for them in that direction. The other six stay here and make sure they haven't hidden in the brush somewhere so they can sneak back to the house while our backs are turned. If anyone asks what's going on, say it's a patrol and ambush exercise in preparation for the battle tomorrow."

Without making a production of it, Melissa went back to work on the ropes around Rep's wrists. Rep felt a sudden letdown, and he sensed that Melissa shared it. Against all the odds, they'd managed to get rid of the guard. They were comparatively safe for—what? The next thirty minutes? Forty-five at the most? At some point, long before twilight, Lawrence was going to think to look in the silo, and he could hardly help finding them when he did. Staying in the silo was the only thing they could have done. It had given them a chance. If they'd run they'd be dead. There was plenty of light, and the muzzle velocity of a Spencer carbine is more than fast enough to negate a two-hundred-second head start, especially with the added burden of Rep's gimpy ankle. But unless Melissa got Rep untied in a hurry they were going to be right back in the soup. All they'd have to show for their improvisation and heroic effort would be a dramatic increase in Peter's survival prospects, for it was inconceivable that Lawrence would risk hanging around much longer after he'd gotten them out of the way.

Rep thought he felt a very slight loosening of one of the cords biting into his wrist. Maybe there was hope after all. Maybe they had a chance. And even if they didn't, their own deaths would still have accomplished something if Peter would just keep his head down for a few more hours.

That's when they heard the bugle.

It was very close—far too close to be coming from the encampment. It came, in fact, Rep realized in astonishment, from the top of the silo. Craning his neck so that he could see through the cracks that the opening roof had created before its motor seized up, he could make out a figure, black against the sunlight, standing at the top of the ladder outside the silo.

The bugle call was *CHARGE!* As a musical instrument, the bugle has severe limitations. Range, tonality, pitch—none of these are outstanding qualities. In one respect, however, it is unequalled. It is loud. Designed to be heard over the clatter of hooves, the rattle of fire from thousands of guns, the roar of cannon, it carries its message a long way.

Voices again came through the door, and this time they were quite clear.

"Whatinhellizat?"

For almost a minute the question had no answer but the penetrating notes of the bugle itself. The ladder was on the side of the silo opposite the door. Someone had to run halfway around the structure and then halfway back to report.

"It's Damon! The guy we're looking for! Up there on toppa that ladder!"

Linda's mouth gaped. She sank to her bottom, ducked her head, and bit into her own knee to keep from screaming.

"Don't shoot him!" Lawrence's voice. "We need him alive! Go up there after him!"

"Hey, what's that?"

"What's what?"

"Something's coming! And they look like they mean it, too!"

"Line up!"

Rep edged over to the doorway, dropped to his belly, and chanced a cautious look through.

"What are they doing?" asked Melissa, who had followed him.

"They're dressing the line," Rep said.

Melissa looked. Lawrence was hastily forming the seventeen men who weren't scurrying up the ladder after Peter into a skirmish line. He wasn't actually barking "Dress right—dress!" but each man lined himself up with the man to his right, then went down on one knee and raised his carbine.

Looking beyond the line, she could see the black cloud racing over the ground a quarter-mile away that had provoked this reaction. No, it wasn't a cloud. And it wasn't black. It was horsemen, at least forty, some in blue and some in gray, sun glinting from the revolvers and sabers in their hands. They were riding—no, they weren't *riding*. They were *galloping* hell for leather, whipping their mounts furiously, digging their spurs into the animals' flanks, racing with heart-stopping abandon toward the bugle's call.

"Dragoons, as I live and breathe," Melissa said.

The charge reminded Rep of a B-52 that he'd seen at an air show once, flying only two hundred feet off the ground. It wasn't just breathtakingly beautiful and terrible at the same time; it was beautiful *because* it was terrible.

Lawrence's let's-pretend soldiers managed one ragged volley. This came when the horsemen were about two hundred feet away—close enough for Rep to recognize Pendleton in the lead, a revolver in each fist and reins clenched between his teeth. A spattering of fire from the charging cavalry answered the carbines. One of Lawrence's men screamed and fell backward, grabbing his side. Another dropped without a sound.

That was all the others needed. Some threw down their guns and raised their hands. The rest broke and ran.

What happened next was quite horrible. Rep remembered a line from Pakenham's history of the Boer War: "The charge of two hundred horsemen galloping across a plain is designed to be an irresistible force. It does not stop simply because the enemy would like to surrender." Three prisoners would be taken this day. *Well*, Rep thought, *bad things happen in war.*

As soon as the line broke Lawrence disappeared from the constricted view Rep and Melissa had. They learned only later that he had run to the blind side of the silo, where Peter was still blowing his bugle at the top of the ladder. Lawrence fired one revolver shot before Peter turned around and noticed him.

Pendleton found Lawrence less than a minute after that, his head burst like a melon by a bugle hurled from a height of forty feet.

◇◇◇

Three hours later, in the reception area at Jackrabbit Press, Linda wiggled her fingers at Peter, who was dressed improbably in a gray uniform and just as improbably handling an oversized cigar. He handed the stogie to her and she took an outlandishly amateurish puff as the prelude to a ragged cough. It was a night when non-smokers did that kind of thing.

"So," Melissa was saying to Henderson, "the reason everyone was all set was that you thought Rep and Linda and I were up to something?"

"Well, sure. I mean, that thing about where can I smoke? Honey, you're talking to an ex-smoker with teenagers. Anyone who gets within sniffing distance of you would know your last cigarette was many showers and mouthwashes ago. So I thought you guys must be planning on meeting Peter out here for some reason, and I figured I'd better get word to Red."

"Thing is," Pendleton said, "Peter had been with me for almost two days. When Karin said that you guys were messing around up here, he got his game face on and insisted on coming up here to make sure everything was all right. I let him do it, and got everyone ready to come on the double if he called us, because the only other thing I could've done was arrest him."

"Why didn't you turn him over to the Kansas City police when he showed up and told you the story?" Rep asked.

"Well, I get a little bit tired of doing *all* those boys' work for 'em. I got them the right saber after they'd done gone an' got the wrong one, and I got it to the lab that found the blood. They were a little cross with me already, so I figured that was enough for someone who was off the clock. The way I saw it, if they wanted me to arrest Peter they should have asked me."

"But didn't they think to look for Peter at the encampment?" Melissa asked.

"That they did, but for some reason they figured he'd be on the Yankee side. I volunteered to look on our side, but somehow I just couldn't turn him up. You know how it is: spend a coupla days jawin' with these city boys and one farmer with bad hair in gray looks pretty much like another one to you."

"Why did you run out here to the encampment?" Linda asked Peter. "Why didn't you just stay with us at the hospital?"

"I thought I was endangering you," Peter said. "It seemed like the best thing to do was tell the story to Red, so he could get the FBI on the thing. I knew Red would trust me not to run off, so he wouldn't have to lock me up. I was afraid Lawrence might be planning some kind of attack to coincide with the re-enactment tomorrow, and I knew Red was the only police officer who'd pay any attention to that. Telling you where I was going would have put you in a tight spot with the police. I just thought you three would have the sense to sit tight."

"Unfortunately," Rep said, "good sense isn't the outstanding characteristic of meddling amateurs who stick their noses in police business."

"That's gospel truth, that is," Pendleton said, playing the cracker-barrel rube shtick for all it was worth. "You can't have a copyright lawyer and a Ph.D. in Literature and a book editor running around doing police work. You've got to let trained police officers figure out that a French poet was a Nazi collaborator and a marathon runner with hospital quality fluid bags must have something more important to do with them than keep his grass fresh and a silo has Baggies inside the top. They would've gotten around to it in two or three years, too, leastwise if no one committed any more murders in the meantime."

Linda pulled Rep a bit shyly away from the laughter surrounding Pendleton, toward a quieter corner of the room.

"Do you think the story is going to break?" she asked. "About Peter and that actress from California?"

"I talked with my, um, my *contact* about half an hour ago," Rep said. "She doesn't think so. She said that only two stringers showed any interest in it after the date-rape drug story got around. They're both lazy, and she said she knows of some microfilm on each of them about things they wouldn't want their moms to see. So she doesn't think they'll pursue it."

"That's a miracle," Linda said.

"That's what my contact said," Rep nodded. "She called it the miracle of the loafs and the fiches."

"It's funny," Melissa said to Rep's back in February of the following year as he lugged a baby car seat down the stairs of the Damons' home. "I didn't pray in the silo. I was scared spitless, and I knew you were scared too, even though we were both keeping up a brave front, but I never thought of praying. Yet for the last month or so I've been praying fervently."

Rep paused at the bottom of the stairs, set the car seat down, and turned to face his wife at the top as she prepared to carry down an overnight bag full of baby clothes. They were on their way to St. Luke's to bring Peter and Linda and their two-day old baby home.

"What were you praying for?" he asked.

"Some kind of bargain basement miracle," she said. "I wanted an angel to come down for a talk with Peter, or something along those lines, so that he'd absolutely *know*, without any shadow of a doubt, that this baby was his."

"I suppose that wouldn't have hurt anything," Rep said, "although it sounds a bit like the type of thing I've seen you make fun of in footnotes now and then."

"Reduction in certainty is a symptom of wisdom. It really started with that woman from Jacks (and Jills!) of All Trades. She told me a story about a miter box her father made for her, and the more I thought about it, the more it seemed to me that it was the first time in my adult life I could imagine the doctrine of the incarnation as anything more than a pretty story."

"You mean in the home of a guy who thinks words are the sound of God laughing you had a carpenter named Jesse Davidovich tell you something that produced a spiritual insight, and you're still looking for angels? How much divine intercession do you think one Ph.D. is entitled to?"

"I'm not sure whether to kiss you or throw this bag at you," she said. "On a topic of this importance, I want all the certainty I can get."

"Take a look at that kid's ears, then," Rep told her. "Because I already have, and I can tell you one thing: his father is either Peter Damon or Prince Charles."

"I pray for a miracle and I get an observant husband with an empiricist attitude," Melissa said.

"Sounds like divine intervention to me," Rep said.

He hoisted the car seat again, momentarily lost his balance under the awkward weight, and grabbed the newel capital with his left hand to steady himself.

It was as solid as a rock.

Bibliographical Note

The text and background of the General Order Number 11 issued on August 25, 1863 at the direction of General Thomas Ewing ("Redlegs") can be found at the Missouri Partisan Ranger website, http://www.rulen.com/partisan/order11.htm.

The text and background of the General Order Number 11 issued on December 17, 1862 at the direction of General Ulysses Grant can be found at the Jewish Virtual Library website, http://www.us-israel.org/jsource/antisemitism/grant.html.

A comprehensive examination of the controversy surrounding the career, trial, and execution of Robert Brassilach and its aftermath is available in *The Collaborator* by Alice Kaplan (The University of Chicago Press 2000). The Brassilach statements quoted or paraphrased in *Unforced Error* are my translations of his actual words as cited in Chapter IV of Bruno Poncharal's French translation of Kaplan's study, *Intelligence avec l'Ennemi: Le Procès Brassilach* (Editions Gallimard 2001). Those statements in the original are, respectively: "Il faut se separer des Juifs en bloc et ne pas garder de petits."; and "…j'ai…même écrit qu'on ne devait pas séparer les femmes des enfants…. "

For details on Civil War weaponry, uniforms, and military terminology, I have relied on Robin Smith and Ron Field, *Uniforms of the Civil War* (The Lyons Press 2001).